BUSTER
The Sheikh of Hope Street

BUSTER
The Sheikh of Hope Street

by Bjarne Reuter
translated by Anthea Bell

DUTTON CHILDREN'S BOOKS
NEW YORK

Library of Congress Cataloging-in-Publication Data

Reuter, Bjarne B.
    [Kys stjernerne. English]
    Buster, the Sheikh of Hope Street / by Bjarne Reuter : translated by
Anthea Bell.—1st American ed.
        p. cm.
    Translation of: Kys stjernerne.
    Summary: The adventures and misadventures of Buster, a highly
imaginative Danish schoolboy, come to a climax when he must take over
the lead role in the school play on the night of the performance.
    ISBN 0-525-44772-5
    [1. Schools—Fiction.   2. Imagination—Fiction.   3. Theater—Fiction.
4. Denmark—Fiction.]   I. Title.
PZ7.R3259Bt   1991   91-19397
[Fic]—dc20   CIP
                                                                     AC

First published in the United States 1991 by Dutton Children's Books,
a division of Penguin Books USA Inc.
375 Hudson Street, New York, New York 10014

Originally entitled *Kys Stjernerne* and published in 1980
by Branner og Korch, Copenhagen, Denmark.

First American Edition   Printed in U.S.A.
10 9 8 7 6 5 4 3 2 1

BUSTER
The Sheikh of Hope Street

with
BUSTER OREGON MORTENSEN

Sheikh Suleiman ◆ Ingeborg
Charlie Mane ◆ The Fairy Elvira
Rosie ◆ Mr. Martinsen ◆ Willy Valdi

also featuring
Anna, Amelia, and Sophie
Benny Lukas Johansen
Jens (and his mother)
Doza Rosa, Mr. Jensen, Allah
Big Lars and Ivor
Dr. Nielsen and Nurse Heidi
Saint Goggelus
the people of Brønshøj
and a large quantity of autumn leaves

CONTENTS

CHAPTER ONE

Charlie Mane and "The Scimitar of the Sheikh"

It was the time of year when leaves decide to change color. And in the Brønshøj marketplace, in the country of Denmark, Wild Victor of Arabia could be seen galloping over Frederikssund Road on his white stallion, Charlie Mane.

You might think the sight of Victor of Arabia galloping along several times a day would create something of a sensation. However, as Victor's real name was Buster Oregon Mortensen and Charlie Mane was made of a broomstick with part of an old horsehair mattress for a head, the sight was not all that sensational. Anyway, most of the people in the marketplace were grown-ups, and as everyone knows, grown-ups are always hurrying somewhere and can't be bothered noticing what goes on around them.

But there were other reasons why today was special. For one thing, the leaves were acquiring dark, warm-looking skins, of the sort old people often have; for another, Willy Valdi, who taught music and singing at Buster's school, had had the brilliant idea of producing a school play. The last few days he had been going around with a thick pad of paper, looking for volunteers. Within two days there were four names on his list, and it would have been five, except Benny Lukas Johansen had to back out because he was going to attend a silver wedding anniversary in Åbenrå the day of the play.

However, the fun really started when the music teacher put up a red poster in the school yard saying what the play would be. It was called *The Scimitar of the Sheikh and the Three Naked Ladies,* so of course crowds of children streamed forward to be in it. But it turned out that the crowds of children had been induced to volunteer under false pretenses.

The play's real name was simply *The Scimitar of the Sheikh*—a student had secretly added *and the Three Naked Ladies* to the poster. That was how Buster Oregon Mortensen came to be entangled in all the excitement of this major theatrical production. Another pupil, a boy by the name of Jens, had let it be known that Buster was responsible for writing in the thing about the naked ladies, whereupon the music teacher told Buster he'd better show up at the first meeting.

Buster was sure he had been asked to come because he was going to be chosen to play the part of Sheikh Suleiman. So he had been practicing riding Charlie Mane all over the place, with elastic bands around the bottoms of his old red conjuror's pants to make them baggy like a desert sheikh's. And when he rode Charlie he always wore his knitted cap backward, so that its peak would protect the nape of his neck from the desert sand.

As Buster galloped into school, Mr. Martinsen, Buster's math teacher, had just wheeled his bike out of the teachers' bicycle shed and was putting his shiny bicycle clips on.

"Whoa there, Charlie, whoa there!" called Buster, tugging at the reins.

Mr. Martinsen stared at Charlie Mane, whose eyes were made of two bright red coat buttons. One of them was rather loose and dangled in the wind. Buster's father said it made Charlie a little cross-eyed.

Mr. Martinsen looked at his watch. It was three-thirty.

"What on earth are you doing in school at this

time of day, Buster Mortensen?" he asked, polishing his shiny handlebars, although they were already gleaming.

Buster tied Charlie to the oak tree in the school yard. He was a little hard of hearing, because his mother said that if he insisted on wearing his cap tipped halfway back on his head like that, he must put cotton in his ears to keep from catching cold.

"Just let me take this cotton out, Mr. Martinsen. It's so I don't get exclamation of the inner ear."

Mr. Martinsen glanced the other way, took a small brown beret out of his pocket, and straightened the little light on his bike.

"Are you going to be in it too?" asked Buster.

"I don't know what you're talking about, boy. If you really must know, I'm going home to correct exercise booklets."

"Your pants look like real desert pants—with the bicycle clips, I mean."

Mr. Martinsen looked down at himself, then swung his leg over the crossbar of his bike. "What's that in your belt?" he asked.

Buster beamed like the sun. "It's a scimitar, Mr. Martinsen."

The math teacher chuckled. "Call that a scimitar? It looks more like a parsley chopper to me."

Buster looked down. "Maybe, but it really is a scimitar."

Mr. Martinsen put his bag in the bike basket. "You know very well you're not allowed to bring that sort of thing to school. It says so in the rules, quite clearly. No knives, daggers, skewers, slingshots, bows and arrows, or air guns. Maybe we ought to add scimitars when the subject next comes up at a staff meeting."

Buster smiled reassuringly. "I only need it for the play," he said. "I'm going to be Sheikh Suleiman, you see, and I thought he'd be kind of a sword-swallower."

"A sword-swallower?" repeated Mr. Martinsen, giving a swallow himself.

"That's right," nodded Buster, stroking Charlie. "Sword-swallowers are greedy pigs, like Charlie Mane here." He was about to mount Charlie, but then he hesitated. "I suppose horseback riding's forbidden in the school yard too, Mr. Martinsen?"

The math teacher bent over his handlebars and pedaled away so fast that he never even noticed the changing color of the leaves.

A great many children had gathered in the gym that afternoon, some of them in beautiful costumes. Jens looked the most spectacular of all.

He had a glittering suit that might have come straight from the exciting pages of *A Thousand and One Nights*. His shoes had long, pointed toes with little bells sewn on them that tinkled as he walked. In his right hand he held a fine sword, and in his left he held the hand of his rather ordinary mother, who smiled at all the other children with a mouth like a closed zipper. (She surely had made him his fancy costume.)

The music teacher told the children to sit down so that he could divide them into four groups. Meanwhile Buster was telling Jens that he had tied up Charlie outside, lest the horse scatter its droppings on the gym floor.

Jens replied that he had never heard of a broomstick that could scatter droppings anywhere.

The meeting took a long time, because it wasn't easy to divide the children into groups. But finally the teacher got it all written down.

"Group one is the actors!" he called. All the children hopped up and down excitedly, and through the cheerful din you could hear the soft tinkling of Jens's shoes. Buster waved to his sister Ingeborg, who was sitting holding her recorder and had no ambition at all to be an actress. There was a great crush around the music teacher because so many kids wanted a big part. Jens's mother fended some of them off, so that Jens's costume wouldn't get crushed. Even so, Buster thought the toe of one shoe was drooping slightly.

"I've jotted down the actors' names," said the teacher. Next he picked the students to be in group two. They were all musicians, including Ingeborg.

Group three was the children who were going to work backstage and make the scenery, and group four contained all those who weren't needed in the play.

"Read the names out!" called Hans, a boy in Buster's class. Hans didn't especially want to be in the play, but it would mean he could skip his after-school chores.

The music teacher mounted a small stool.

"I've picked Jens to play Sheikh Suleiman," said the teacher. "Maurice and Eric will be his faithful henchmen. Anna, Amelia, and Sophie will be the ladies of the harem, and Rosie will play Princess Goldilocks."

A deep sigh passed through the room. Almost everyone looked at Jens, who glanced happily at his mother, who unzipped her mouth. But Buster was looking at Rosie, who was blowing a big bubble with her bubble gum. He thought she was very pretty, with skin so clear it seemed almost like glass. She had two barrettes in her blond hair, and she hardly seemed to have noticed that she was going to be the Princess Goldilocks.

Buster went up to the teacher. "I didn't hear which group you said I was in," he told him, smearing his freshly chalked moustache all over his face.

"You're the boy who wrote on my poster, right?" The teacher glanced at his notebook.

"That was just to get people to come to the meeting. . . ."

"Right, right. Nevertheless, you go in group four, Buster Mortensen," said the music teacher, putting the little stool back where it belonged. "All the actors can come and collect their parts now!" he called. "And tomorrow I'll tell the stagehands and musicians what they have to do!"

The meeting was over. Ingeborg and Buster were the last to leave. Buster untied Charlie Mane.

"You're all black in the face!" observed Ingeborg.

"It's my moustache," explained Buster, watching Jens march proudly across the school yard with his script.

Buster bent down and slipped the elastic bands off his pant legs.

"Nine leaves had fallen off that elm when I arrived," he said. "There are sixteen on the ground now. Can you walk Charlie home, Ingeborg? I have to go to the dairy."

Ingeborg explained that she had to go into town on the way home, and it wouldn't be very easy to take Charlie Mane with her.

The music teacher came striding by, on his way to the parking lot. He stopped when he saw Ingeborg and Buster.

"By the way, Buster," he said, "one of the pieces of scenery is very big—it's one of the flats—and we'll need an extra person to push it on and off. Would you like to do the job?"

Buster's face lit up. "You bet I would!" he cried. "Great! Terrific!"

The teacher nodded and unlocked his car. Shortly afterward the school yard was completely empty except for the autumn leaves still lying there. Buster was staring into space, grinning to himself. Then he gave Ingeborg a quick kiss on the cheek and mounted Charlie. He rode around the yard ten times, singing:

Charlie Mane,
Charlie Mane,
A handsome horse and strong,
Gallops over deserts
Taking me along.
If you think I'm lying,
Let me say to you:
All the desert sands
Are true as they are—yellow!

Ingeborg went down the steps, waving to him as he disappeared through the school gate. Then she sat down on the bottom step and took out her recorder.

CHAPTER TWO

The Fairy Elvira from the Underground Land

"Never mind making excuses for him, I won't have any fooling around in my shop. As if there were customers lined up outside fighting to get in! As if a person made a fortune selling yogurt and margarine! As if life was just a bed of roses!"

"Your blood pressure!" The dairyman's wife was trying to calm Mr. Jensen down. "Remember your blood pressure, do, Jensen!"

The fat dairyman marched around the counter.

"Don't you bother about my blood pressure, don't you bother about anything. Just go off to the hairdresser and get your bangs cut, and then maybe there'll be somebody else around here that can see two inches in front of their nose. So my blood pressure's too high, is it? Well, let me tell you, I'm seething inside, and why, I ask you, why? As if life was easy, as if there wasn't trouble enough anyway! As if life was worth living!"

Jensen went back to the refrigerator shelves.

"We can't keep him on, and that's that. . . . No need for you to start whimpering, Marie. Just look at those milk cartons. When did he do it? Did you see him do it? Yesterday, was it?"

"I don't know," sniffled Mrs. Jensen.

Jensen hysterically bit his knuckles.

"Milk cartons are supposed to look all the same. I can't have that crazy boy painting faces on them. Come here, Marie, see that carton of sour cream with sunglasses? Who d'you think that looks like? And the carton of buttermilk up in the corner sticking its tongue out—oh, God, give me strength. I . . . I . . ." Mr. Jensen suddenly froze. For a moment he simply stared out the window.

It was raining outside. The rain was dripping rhythmically through the three holes in the awning that he had mended last autumn. Then Mrs. Jensen saw what her husband was staring at.

"What on earth is that between his legs?" stammered Mr. Jensen.

"Something between his legs, is there?" murmured Mrs. Jensen timidly, looking out the window.

Buster rode four times round the hydrants and

then tied Charlie Mane to the hook meant for dogs on leashes. He walked through the gate and into the courtyard of the little dairy, whistling. A couple of minutes later he could be heard moving about in the room behind the shop. Mr. Jensen didn't like Buster to use the shop door. He wanted it left for his customers.

Buster came into the shop carrying a wire basket. Mrs. Jensen smiled nervously at him but said nothing. Mr. Jensen was still staring out the window.

"Just what have you tied up to that hook outside the shop?" he groaned.

Buster went over to the window. "Oh, that's only Charlie Mane, Mr. Jensen," he said.

"Charlie Mane?" repeated Mr. Jensen.

Buster explained proudly that Charlie was his horse. Then he casually mentioned the school play he was going to be in.

With an expression on his face like a sleepwalker's, the dairyman went over to the big refrigerator and pointed to the cartons.

"Explain that," he said.

Buster smiled. "Well, it was like this. I thought since they're called sour cream or sweet cream, they ought to look sour or sweet too, so I brought my crayons and I—"

"Get out!"

"But—"

"Out, I said!"

Mrs. Jensen took a step forward.

Buster looked from one to the other of them.

Mr. Jensen did not mince his words. "You're fired, Buster Mortensen. Is that clear? Sacked, finished, all washed up here, so get out, shove off. . . ."

Buster backed toward the door.

"And take that broomstick with you."

Outside, Buster took off his knitted cap and wrung it out.

Charlie's eyes were dripping with rainwater. He looked as if he were crying.

Buster turned and glanced at the window of the dairy. It was foggy with condensation. Then he mounted Charlie and rode to the marketplace, where he found an awning to stand under, one without any holes in it.

After a few minutes he saw Mr. Larsen coming out of a florist's near the church.

"Hi, Mr. Larsen!" he shouted cheerfully.

"Hi, Buster! Hi, Charlie!" Mr. Larsen shouted back.

Buster rode over to him. "Those are lovely flowers you've bought today," he said. "She'll like those."

14

"I hope so," murmured Mr. Larsen, looking into space. "Want to come along?"

Buster nodded. They passed the minister's house and went into the cemetery. Buster told Mr. Larsen he had just been fired for drawing faces on milk cartons. But on the other hand, he had this terrific job in the school play.

Mr. Larsen smiled.

"That's life," he said. "Ups and downs, ins and outs. Are you going to play the dashing sheikh of Arabia?"

Buster explained that his job was even more important.

Mr. Larsen nodded. "Good stagehands are very important indeed," he agreed seriously.

They had reached the corner of the cemetery where a small white marble tombstone with a dove on it bore the name of Mrs. Ingrid Larsen. Mrs. Larsen had been a very good friend to Buster.

As usual, they stood there for a while, just looking at the stone. Then Mr. Larsen bent down and got to work with his little rake. But it was raining so hard he couldn't do much.

Buster thought it was a beautiful grave.

Mr. Larsen left his little bunch of flowers in a cemetery vase that he sunk into the ground.

"The rain will do them good," he said, red in the face from bending. He swept a few autumn leaves off the slab. "Ah, well," he said. "We'll all go the same way."

Buster nodded. Mr. Larsen always talked like that.

"Will you join Mrs. Larsen again when you die?" he asked.

Mr. Larsen looked at him and put an arm around his shoulders. His coat smelled of earth and mildew. Buster liked the smell.

"Maybe," said Mr. Larsen. "Who knows? That'll be decided elsewhere. Decisions about you are always made elsewhere."

Buster looked up at him. "Do they decide elsewhere if I can spit on the path here?"

"Spit on the path?" said Mr. Larsen. "Why do you want to spit on the path all of a sudden?"

"Because I've got a bug or something in my mouth."

Mr. Larsen smiled and gave Buster a quick hug. Then they left the cemetery, and Buster fished the bug out of his mouth.

"What do you think about when you stand beside your wife's grave?" asked Buster as they passed the church.

"What do I think about? Hm," murmured Mr. Larsen. "Well, I suppose I think of her, Ingrid, and how it was when we were together. Before she got sick. There's a lot of things to think

16

about when you're coming near the end. Life seems endlessly long to you, Buster, but it seems very, very short to me."

Buster nodded. "Like going home at the end of the vacation."

"Going home at the end of the vacation?"

"Yes, the trip home always goes very quickly."

"That's right," said Mr. Larsen seriously. "Yes, there's something in what you say."

They reached the dark red gate. Buster stopped and faced Mr. Larsen. "Do you still love her, Mr. Larsen?"

"Do I still love her, Buster? Why, sure, but she's dead."

"Can't you love her even if she's dead?"

Mr. Larsen put his arm around Buster. "Well now, that's the funny thing, Buster," he said into Buster's knitted cap. "It's only now she's gone I realize how much I actually did love her."

Buster nodded. He understood.

They were going in the direction of the bar. Mr. Larsen stopped at its door. "Well, Buster Oregon Mortensen, the fact is, old Larsen here has a dry throat. Must be all that water pouring down from God's heaven. So I have to stop here a minute. Maybe you could ride off to the new supermarket and buy me a packet of cigarettes and something for supper? Something easy to cook, okay? Think you can do that, Buster?"

Buster thought he could certainly do that.

"And buy yourself something too, a chocolate frog, how about that?" Chocolate frogs were Buster's favorite candy.

"I'm afraid I'd have to buy two, Mr. Larsen," said Buster regretfully.

"How come?"

"Well, you know what Charlie's like. He can't bear to see somebody eating if he has to go hungry himself."

Mr. Larsen stared at Buster in surprise. "Well, fancy that, Buster!"

Buster shook his head sadly.

"And does he by any chance like chocolate frogs?" asked Mr. Larsen.

Buster sighed and mounted Charlie. "He's crazy about them. The only horse I ever knew that was."

Buster could still remember when there had been a small general store and a bakery and a butcher shop where the supermarket now was. His father had told him that fifteen years ago, a movie theater had stood on the site. It was called the Bella Cinema. Every Sunday afternoon there would be long lines of fidgeting children waiting to see Hopalong Cassidy and Wild West movies.

If it was a really good movie, you had to stand in line for two hours. People still stood in line there today, but at the supermarket checkout counters instead. Sometimes Buster imagined that the Bella Cinema, with all the snotty-nosed children and Wild West movies, had simply sunk into the ground and lay underneath the supermarket, ready to come up again one fine day like snowflakes springing up from the frozen ground.

However, he liked the supermarket. It was always nice and warm in there, and there was always music. It was like going into a living room. An amazing living room, with eighteen checkout counters and ladies sitting at all the cash registers wearing orange smocks and shiny nameplates. Not showing their whole names, just their initials and last names. They probably didn't want people to call them by their first names.

And Buster would have admitted that he had a special reason for liking the supermarket. There was a lady called E. Laursen who sat at checkout counter 16. She had short red hair and a very small nose and two pointed ears that stuck out sideways. Her green eyes looked as if they were in the middle of a blue lake, because E. Laursen wore so much eye makeup that you felt quite dazzled looking at her. As if her eyes were two spots of sunlight on a shining lake.

Buster had never seen anything so beautiful. Her fingers were long and slim, and her nails were varnished the same color as her hair. If you went to the supermarket late in the afternoon the nail varnish was a little chipped, but she worked so fast you hardly noticed. No one in the world could put frozen chicken into plastic bags as fast as E. Laursen. All her movements were so swift and sure that Buster, watching, sometimes forgot about himself and everything around him. When the customers paid, she smiled, showing her teeth, which were white except for one that was made of pure gold. But even when she smiled she almost never looked at people; she looked away quickly at her cash register, as if something made her feel uneasy.

She was the fastest of all the cashiers, and Buster was sure she was a fairy. Not because she was so pretty and had pointed ears, but because she couldn't speak. He had been to the supermarket at least fifty times, and he had gone to checkout counter 16 every time, and she had never spoken a single word.

He was sure her first name was Elvira, and that when the supermarket closed she made herself invisible and went to the Underground Land of Hopalong Cassidy and Ivanhoe and the knights with their castles, deep, deep down to a time when movie tickets cost less than half what they cost now. Where else would she go? He had watched every evening for two weeks after finishing work in the dairy, and at quarter past six exactly the other seventeen cashiers came out. But never Elvira the silent fairy.

Buster took a basket, walked past the long shelves, and found a can of mock turtle soup that only had to be heated up. Mr. Larsen could probably manage that.

He chose two licorice sticks for himself, and he got the cigarettes at the machine in the front of the supermarket. Then at last he could stand in line at counter 16, where Elvira was juggling with mustard pickles, dog food, and toothpicks on sale. Buster unloaded his stuff. He knew she had a little lever to step on under her seat to help her move the goods along, and he knew she had seen him, because she was already smiling.

Buster, still mounted on Charlie Mane, felt more like the dashing Sheikh Suleiman than an ordinary stagehand.

His turn came at last, but everything was very busy and hurried. He always felt flustered when it came to paying, because things happened so fast. He was just going to put his purchases in a bag when he heard a loud scream beside him.

Everyone froze, even Elvira. Buster was about

to turn and see what had happened when the scream came again, even louder. Now he realized that everyone was looking at him, and to his astonishment Elvira suddenly got off her little swivel chair, came round to him, Buster, and grabbed Charlie.

Buster beamed like the sun. But it seemed Charlie was the cause of all the trouble. Unfortunately, the broomstick that was Charlie's body had poked itself under a lady's coat when Buster bent down, and matters were not improved when he turned to see what was wrong. Half of Charlie was still between the lady's legs. She herself was lying on top of Italian tomatoes that were rolling about among the checkout counters.

Luckily Elvira came and freed the lady from the broomstick and the tomatoes. A man began picking the tomatoes up. The lady was red in the face and sputtering that she had never known anything like it. Several other ladies glared at Buster and shook their heads.

Buster, at a loss for words, clutched Charlie's bridle and watched Elvira help the upset ladies out through the glass doors. Then she came back to her little chair. But just before turning to serve the next customer she looked straight at Buster and winked.

At that Buster gave Charlie free rein. Away they went at a gallop. Out into the rain, over to the bar, where Mr. Larsen said he really wouldn't be doing much more gambling, and down Church Road, where Buster could give Charlie his head. He ended up standing all by himself on a hill in the pouring rain, looking happily out over Utterslev Park.

"Elvira!" he shouted.

So although one of Charlie's eyes might still be dangling slightly loose, although Buster was only going to be a stagehand, although he had been fired from his job this wet, rainy day, life was all right. He laughed out loud as he galloped down the road, across the park, and home to Hope Street, where Ingeborg was sitting up in their attic bedroom practicing her recorder.

"Take it easy!" she said as Buster burst in.

"It's raining cats and dogs!" he gasped, parking Charlie on the chest of drawers.

"That's no reason to break the door down."

Buster put his dripping jeans over the radiator. Ingeborg went back to practicing the recorder.

"It's shrunk," said Buster.

"What's shrunk?"

"It always does in the rain. You wouldn't know, of course, Ingeborg."

Ingeborg glanced at him, resignedly. "What on earth are you talking about?"

"My weenie. It sort of creeps back into itself. Look."

Ingeborg giggled and turned her back to him. "You've been out in the rain plenty of times, right?"

Buster pulled on some dry clothes, then came and laid his head against her ponytail.

"Oh, go away, you pest!"

"What?" yelled Buster, jumping on the bed and turning somersaults. "How dare you call me a pest—me, the great Buster Oregon Mortensen, top stagehand of the whole world, the boy whose grandfather was fired out of a cannon as tall as a tower, and who's been fired himself, come to think of it, by a dairyman as fat as his own butter. Okay, you just listen to me, my innocent little Ingeborg: If you're very lucky, and you clean the spit out of your recorder, and you do the dishes instead of me this evening, I'll tell you the wonderful tale of the underground fairy Elvira who sits at checkout counter sixteen."

Whereupon Buster took a great leap and landed right in front of Ingeborg.

"Okay, Buster," she said calmly. "But you can do the dishes yourself. And take your foot off my music stand!"

24

CHAPTER THREE

A Heap of
Autumn Leaves

Buster was on his way to school, and he was not in a hurry. It was fine weather. The sky seemed to have climbed a story higher and turned a shade more blue.

Now he began to walk faster. It was a good day, because his class teacher, Rosa Hansen—who didn't mind too much if they called her Rosa and sometimes added Doza for fun—had said they could spend the first two lessons today decorating the classroom. Buster had woken up early, and an idea had occurred to him as day dawned outside. It was a wonderful idea. It kept him laughing all the way down to the row of linden trees. As he expected, there were piles of autumn leaves lying there, and within five minutes he had collected such a big heap he could hide in it.

He looked at the leaves. Some of them were

yellow, others brown, still others dark red. They would look great pasted on a sheet of gray wrapping paper. The only problem was carrying them. He couldn't put them in his schoolbag, because it had had a big hole in it for the last six months—Buster took good care that that hole was never mended. It was very useful when there was arithmetic or Danish homework. "Sorry, Mr. Martinsen, it's that stupid hole," he would say. "My math homework must have fallen out on the way." But now he could have used a proper bag.

Then he got the idea of stuffing the leaves under his coat. He might put a few under his knitted cap too—they'd help to keep him warm as well.

Buster stuffed the dry leaves all over himself. Some of them went down the legs of his jeans, others went up his sleeves. By the time he was finished he looked like a living scarecrow. He laughed and ran around the almost leafless linden tree three times.

Big Lars and his friend Ivor were standing not far away. They had left school last year, and most of the time they just hung around at loose ends. Sometimes they took apart Lars's moped, and then they would spend a couple of hours putting it back together again. They enjoyed that.

When they were through they were filthy and looked very dangerous. That's when they would lie in wait for schoolchildren.

On such days a lot of kids got scolded for coming home with oil on the backs of their necks. Gradually the smaller children learned to avoid Lars and Ivor, and if they happened to come home all black and dirty—but not because they had met the two big boys—they'd just say, "It was Big Lars and Ivor. They always push us around and mess us up when we come out of school!"

Mostly, however, Lars and Ivor had other things to do. For instance, they liked to hang out at the snack bar and kid around with Wong Siao Lo, who was learning Danish.

This morning, however, they had been at work on an upside-down garden table, breaking a Y-shaped steel bracket off its frame. Ivor had been quick to see that this bracket would make a powerful slingshot, and luckily he also had a lot of metal rivets in his pocket. He and Lars were now shooting at a sea gull's tail, although they were growing a little bored because they kept missing. Suddenly Ivor grabbed Lars by the sleeve.

"What on earth is that waddling along?" he said.

Big Lars took his sunglasses off. "It looks blown up like a balloon," he said.

Ivor laughed nastily and fitted a rivet into the slingshot. He stretched the elastic way back. "Let's see if we can make our waddling friend move any faster!" he said, laughing.

The rivet hit Buster in the middle of his back, but he just shuffled on.

"Missed," said Lars. "Pass me the slingshot and dry your tears. I'll show you how to pepper the little dumpling."

Big Lars took the slingshot and pulled on the elastic till it nearly broke. *Whoosh* . . . the rivet whistled through the air and buried itself deep in Buster's coat.

Still nothing happened. Buster simply plodded on.

Ivor stared at Lars. Lars stared at the slingshot.

"There's something funny going on here," said Big Lars. "I'm sure I hit him!"

At that moment Buster turned around. Ivor groaned.

"It's him! It's that weirdo Buster."

Big Lars glanced at the slingshot, then threw it aside. "I could use an egg roll," he said. "With plenty of mustard."

"Why weren't we born someplace else, in

some other time?" groaned Ivor. "Come on, Lars, maybe we can let the air out of a few bicycle tires along the way—that usually helps."

Buster went into his classroom. He was twenty minutes early, and it was very quiet in the school. I'm the only person in this whole school, he thought. But the next moment a small lady came tripping down the corridor. She looked very tired and didn't notice Buster, who had never seen her before. I guess she goes to night school, he said to himself, and maybe they kept her after class last night and she couldn't go home till now.

In a little while the other children showed up, and when the bell rang, Rosa came hurrying in and announced they couldn't decorate the classroom until tomorrow. Now they all had to go and be examined by the school nurse, because nits had been found in the classroom.

"Don't take your coats off," Rosa told them. "Line up in pairs and follow me."

Buster looked down at himself. A few leaves were showing, sticking out of his shoes. They hurt him under his arms.

The children had to wait outside the nurse's office, because Rosa wanted a word with the doctor first. She told them they mustn't talk, or run around, or hit each other. Kurt asked if he could eat the snack he had brought for recess, but Rosa said it was only ten past eight and he should wait.

Amelia stared at Buster. "You do look funny," she said.

Buster was about to explain that he had thought it was today they'd be decorating the classroom, but Jens butted in. "Hey, what've you padded yourself with, Buster?" he asked. "Rosa said we mustn't keep secrets from one other, so come on, tell us!"

Buster looked at them. Caroline and Anders had joined the group. Now that he thought about it, he didn't really feel like telling them he was all padded out with linden leaves. So he said he had done some deep breathing first thing in the morning, and he happened to breathe too deeply and suddenly went all fat like this.

"You're a terrible liar!" Sarah scoffed.

"You said it!" Jens made a face and then retreated so that Buster couldn't reach him. "And you have nits!"

All the other kids hopped around when Jens said "nits," repeating it. "Nits, nits, nits . . ." Then Rosa suddenly appeared in the corridor. She grabbed hold of Amelia, and Amelia said she had only said "nits" once, and it was mean and horrible and unfair if she had to be punished when Jens had been the one who started it. But Jens said Buster started it, and finally Rosa made Buster go into the nurse's office first.

Buster went in. He was feeling rather uneasy. That was because anyone who got hurt or had a nosebleed went to see Nurse Heidi, who would hand out Band-Aids or iodine, and the injured child would leave with a large hard candy in his or her mouth. "To make it feel better," Nurse Heidi would say. And that was why Buster had let himself fall down in a faint outside the teachers' office one Thursday morning.

He had had to lie there all through recess, because the teachers going in and out just stepped over him. Finally Mr. Martinsen had come along and told him to stand up.

Buster had controlled himself.

"I said stand up, Buster Mortensen!" Mr. Martinsen had ordered him.

Luckily Mrs. Møller had come along. Mrs. Møller made the teachers' coffee, had weak legs, and rode a large tricycle. Buster was very glad she had come along just then.

Sure enough, Mrs. Møller had thought Buster looked really pale and said she guessed he had fainted.

"Him, faint?" Mr. Martinsen had prodded

Buster with the toe of his shoe. "He didn't faint. He's got the audacity to lie down right in front of the door to the office with the photocopying machine! What nerve!"

So then Buster had groaned and done his clever trick of rolling his eyes back so that you could only see the whites.

Mrs. Møller, who had been about to get a Danish pastry, shrieked, and then things had started happening very fast. Rosa was called, and suddenly the custodian was there too, and they had carried Buster upstairs to Nurse Heidi and put him on the black couch in the nurse's office.

Then his only problem was how to come around. He couldn't just open his eyes and groan, "Where am I?" He thought it might be better to talk in a rambling sort of way. So when Nurse Heidi had closed the door behind Rosa and the others, Buster had murmured, "Oh, oh . . . my mouth . . . it's so dry. . . ."

The nurse's aide came hurrying up with a glass of water. "Here, dear," she said, "drink this."

Buster had sipped the water. But then Nurse Heidi had said she thought she'd better call an ambulance, and a moment later Buster opened his eyes. He immediately spotted the jar of candies on the big desk.

Although he had staggered like anything as he dragged himself over to the door, and although he had stood there for ages fumbling with the handle, the lid had stayed closed on the jar of candies. Ever since then Nurse Heidi gave him a peculiar look if she happened to meet him in the hallway.

Which was why Buster didn't think it was such a good idea right now to be going in to see Nurse Heidi and Dr. Nielsen with leaves stuffed under his clothes.

Luckily Rosa was there too.

"You can put your things on that chair," said Nurse Heidi.

Buster looked down at himself.

"I . . . er . . . well . . ."

"Didn't you hear? Take your coat off," Rosa told him.

Buster nodded and took his coat off.

Soon afterward he had taken his jeans off too. And then his yellow African shirt with the lions on it. Finally he was standing there in his underpants in the middle of a great heap of autumn leaves.

He remembered that he had some linden leaves stuffed inside his knitted cap, so he took that off as well. "I think that's it," he whispered.

Dr. Nielsen and Nurse Heidi looked at Rosa, who went red in the face.

"Would you fetch a dustpan and broom, Nurse?" asked Dr. Nielsen. "Or no, on second thought, I think you'd better fetch the custodian and ask him to bring a garbage bag with him. A large garbage bag!"

Nurse Heidi nodded and went out.

Dr. Nielsen glanced at Rosa. "If you'll see that the children out there in the corridor keep quiet, Miss Hansen, I'd like a word with this young man."

Rosa nodded, and she went out too.

Dr. Nielsen picked up a green file. Buster saw that it was labeled "B. Mortensen." At the same time he remembered the scar Ingeborg had painted on his back yesterday evening. It ran all the way from his neck to his bottom.

"Come here," said Dr. Nielsen, without looking at him.

Buster stepped out of the pile of leaves and went over to the doctor, who was reading his file.

"Meningitis aged one . . . hm, yes . . . suspected concussion in second grade after falling off flagpole, hospitalized for observation. . . . Can you hear what I'm saying, Buster?"

Buster nodded vigorously. The doctor was carefully studying his papers.

"It says here you were almost completely deaf in both ears when you had a medical examination last year."

"That was because I'd just had conflagration of the middle deer," explained Buster.

The doctor looked at him openmouthed. "Conflagration of the middle deer?"

"Yes, and both my ears were lanced to the drumsticks. The doctor on emergency duty did it."

"You mean you had inflammation of the middle ear?"

"That's right. Inflammation of the middle ear."

"Did this inflammation of the middle ear make you deaf?"

"No, but, well, it's like this. . . . The day of the medical examination I forgot I had cotton in my ears."

Dr. Nielsen closed the green file and looked hard at Buster.

"You're not a bad boy, are you, Buster Mortensen?"

Buster shook his head.

"Not trying to play a practical joke on us, Buster, are you?"

"No," whispered Buster.

"All right. Then turn around."

Buster turned slowly and heard Dr. Nielsen draw his breath in sharply.

"What kind of a scar is that?"

Buster explained that Ingeborg had painted it on because they were playing a game about Arabs in the Underground Land.

"Do you have lice at home?" growled the doctor.

"Lice?" repeated Buster.

"Lice. Nits. Little creatures swarming around."

"I once had guppies swarming around an aquarium, but—"

"That's enough out of you!" shouted Dr. Nielsen.

Just then the custodian arrived with a large paper bag. Dr. Nielsen asked him to take Buster away with him.

Outside, the others were sitting with Rosa, working on their reading books. Amelia was just telling Rosa she had brought some posters they could put up in the classroom. And Jens was saying his dad could get hold of some pictures of old ships, worth a lot of money.

In fact everyone had brought something along to decorate the classroom. Rosa said it was going to look really great by the time they were through.

Buster put his gray knitted cap on his head and pulled it right down over his ears. That way they might not ask him what *he* had brought.

But as the lessons went on he sidled over to Rosa and said he knew a man called Mr. Larsen who had a stuffed parrot they could have for the classroom. Rosa said that was a terrific idea; perhaps the parrot could sit on the desk where everyone could see it. Buster smiled at her and thought he might just as well wait a while before telling her about the plastic bag you had to put over the stuffed bird because it smelled so bad.

CHAPTER FOUR

The Listening Stars

Buster was standing outside the Brønshøj bar. It was late. So late that the volume was turned down all over the town.

He had gone along the empty streets of fine big houses between Hope Street and Church Road, streets where the houses stood neatly in silent rows, their windows shuttered. All the little old men would be lying in their warm beds snuggling up to their wives' fat tummies, Buster had thought, chuckling. Some of them would be grinding their teeth, and others would be smacking their lips.

But the stars were always there. They were shining brightly tonight as Buster trudged up Church Road. He thought that the stars were probably listening to the thoughts of sleepless people and then whispering to each other, and that the round Man in the Moon had just smiled as he swallowed another cloud of smoke.

Even from a long way off Buster could hear the noise in the bar. Someone was singing, loudly. A harmonica was playing in the background. Buster smiled. He knew it was his father playing.

"You'd better go and get him," his mother had said. "Or he won't be home till tomorrow and we'll have trouble with him all day."

Buster had gone on this errand before, and every time, his father said it would be the last time. The reason his mother never went was that she knew it would embarrass his father too much. Everyone made jokes about it. Anyway, Buster's father believed a bar was no place for his wife.

Buster went in. Although it was late, there were still a lot of customers around. Mr. Larsen had once said, "There are more of us all the time. What else can we do?"

Only one woman was there. That is to say, it was someone called Dolores, but she wasn't really a woman, she was a man dressed up. Her real name was Dennis. Her red lips shone through the heavy pall of smoke. She was leaning against the juke box in its tall, lilac-colored neon casing. She looked as if she wanted to melt into it.

Buster had once been in love with the waitress, whose name was Asta. She sashayed her way from table to table, eyes red, avoiding the arms that went out to catch hold of her.

"Keep your paws off my behind, Arnold!" she told Benny's father while a little cloud of beer foam fell on Mr. Larsen's head. Mr. Larsen was too lost in thought to say anything.

Buster waved to his father, and his father immediately stood up, stretching his arms out.

"My son, my son!" he cried happily, and all the others greeted Buster and tried to catch hold of him. Buster, however, went straight up to his father, who picked him up, put him on a table, and called for silence.

"Here you see," uttered Buster's father gravely, "the sole survivor of a world catastrophe no one's even noticed yet!"

Many of the men nodded, solemnly.

Asta dried her hands on her apron and shouted, "Stop that drunken nonsense!"

"Look out the window, my girl!" urged Buster's father.

"You'd better go home," advised Asta, and Buster's father nodded and took Buster off the table again.

"Hadn't we better take Mr. Larsen with us?" asked Buster.

40

Asta gave him a hug.

"Larsen's gone away," murmured his father. "Far, far away into space, where the galaxies meet and dreams begin and end."

Buster looked at Mr. Larsen, who was sitting on a chair with a peculiar, empty expression on his face.

Asta slipped Buster a coin.

"Hey, we must be lovers again!" laughed Buster.

"Dear me, your sort of love can't be bought for money!" cried Asta, throwing her head back. Then she placed her right foot on Mr. Larsen's chair and sang:

> Who's the fairest of the fair,
> little man, I sigh,
> known for beauty everywhere
> underneath the sky?
>
> Who has eyes like stars at night
> in the misty land?
> She wants no gold or silver bright,
> she only wants your hand.

"My mother's the fairest of the fair!" declared Buster, who had often heard this song of Asta's before.

Asta sat down on Mr. Larsen's lap.

"Give us another!" called Dolores from the back of the room.

"Give me a new pair of feet!" groaned Asta. "Though come to think of it, this place would be just about unbearable but for my poor feet—at least they stop me from feeling sorry for all you drunks!"

"Give us another song, go on!" shouted another man.

Buster and his father left.

"The beer's gone to my legs," chuckled Buster's father, leaning on Buster.

It was very cold. Buster buttoned up his coat and produced a purple scarf. "Here, put this on or you'll catch your death of cold," he said.

His father looked at the long scarf. It had letters of the alphabet embroidered on it, yellow and bright red. Buster bit his lip expectantly. The scarf, and the wording on it, were a surprise for his father.

"The Great Osman from Osmania," read his father. "The Great Osman from Osmania." That had been his name when he performed as a magician and strongman.

They were so far from Church Road by now that the noise from the bar had dwindled to a distant hum.

Buster's father clutched the scarf close to him. He looked very serious. Perhaps he was cold. At any rate his nose was running slightly.

"When did you make that?" he asked.

"Well . . . Ingeborg helped me a bit," said Buster.

"It's very, very beautiful. Very," said his father, winding the scarf four times around his neck. Then he took his shiny harmonica out of his pocket and played a thin little tune that he said was a flying carpet. At the first note they took off and flew to the sound of the music, soaring high above all the little old men and their fat wives and down to Hope Street, where they slipped in through the door of their apartment building like two quiet cats.

"Tomorrow," said Buster's father, "tomorrow we'll finish building our ship, right, Buster?"

Buster nodded and helped his father into the living room.

"Tomorrow we'll hoist her sails!" murmured his father, lying down on the sofa.

"Then you won't be going to the bar tomorrow?" whispered Buster, undoing his father's coat.

His father shook his head and tried to sit up. "I'm never going to the bar again," he said.

Buster took his father's trousers off. "Don't

forget what you just promised," he whispered, fetching his father a pillow.

"I love you, Buster," said his father, waving both hands.

"Okay, but keep quiet or you'll wake Mom," Buster warned.

Then he went up to the attic bedroom, where Ingeborg had moved the bed around. Its head now stood against the narrow end of the room. That meant winter had come. They could expect snow in a month's time. It sounded so good when the snow slid off the roof.

Buster undressed and left his clothes in a heap beside the bed. Charlie Mane's head lay on the chair where he usually put his clothes. He put on his pajamas, smiling, and then looked serious. Tomorrow—tomorrow they had a math test. What had Mr. Martinsen said? "If I were you children I'd practice my multiplication tables really thoroughly." Multiplication tables! Oh, help! Multiplication tables were important. Buster dropped heavily onto the side of the bed. Amelia had told him her big sister knew her tables up to seventeen times—by heart. Buster did not know how old Amelia's big sister was, but anyway she must be a very happy girl. Imagine knowing up to your seventeen times table!

He scrambled into bed next to the sleeping Ingeborg. She had put clean sheets on the bed. Buster could tell that the covers had been hanging out of doors all day. You could almost smell the autumn wind in them. The sheets crackled slightly. He blew his nose thoroughly. Except for the multiplication tables he would have been feeling very, very good.

"Ingeborg," he whispered, "are you asleep?"

It seemed she was. Her back was turned toward him, and he had to listen hard to hear her breathing.

"I've brought you back a dream," he said. "About Elvira. And Sheikh Suleiman, and all the prophets of Arabia with their long beards."

He put his mouth close to her ear.

"First of all Asta the belly dancer enters. You can see that her feet hurt her, but she smells good under her arms because she puts deodorant on every couple of hours. She has a bottle cap in her navel. Dr. Nielsen and Nurse Heidi are sitting behind her. They're just visiting, selling fallen leaves in the Sahara.

"They watch Asta dance on burning coals. At least, they think they're burning coals—they're really licorice-flavored candies. Then the sheikh enters all of a sudden. He looks like a boy from

Brønshøj. A boy with amazing muscles. He's riding a fiery white steed with blue spots. There's a little boy sitting in one corner sucking the toe of his pointy shoe. His mom's with him.

"Suddenly everything goes quiet in the big tent. Dr. Nielsen and Nurse Heidi huddle together, Asta pulls her belly in, and scimitars are drawn. The dashing Sheikh Abdullah el Hassan del Mortensen waves his pointed hat above his dark head and everyone falls silent. At last the sheikh speaks. 'What's nine times six?' he asks. They all look down, but no one can tell him the answer to nine times six. So he calls, 'Bring in the prisoner!'

"Two strong men and a big strong woman drag the ugly villain of the oasis into the tent, and everyone cries out in amazement. It is the white slave driver Mr. Martinsen. But the sheikh is stronger than he is, and he makes the villain do a rain dance on the six-sided licorice candies, and then they tickle the soles of the slave driver's feet until he dies laughing."

Buster lay back on his own pillow.

"Oh, and did I tell you I don't have nits, Ingeborg? Well, obviously I don't. How would they live in the desert at a temperature of forty degrees?"

Then he smacked his lips three times and closed his eyes . . . so he never saw the moonbeam that struck Charlie Mane's eye right then, making it glow in the darkness of the room.

And then a cloud sailed in front of the moon, and soon Buster was asleep with his mouth open, and the only thing to be seen in the bedroom were his black fingernails on the white coverlet.

CHAPTER FIVE

A Pen and a Window

Mr. Martinsen put a pile of gray exercise booklets on the desk in front of him. A small muscle began twitching under his right eye. The whole class sat in front of him expectantly with nothing on their desks but their pencil cases. It was two minutes past nine.

Buster looked out the window for a moment, at the school yard and the playing field. The low wooden fence had been replaced by a steel chainlink fence three meters high, with a wavy line of steel wire on top. It already looked rusty, even though it had been up only a few months.

Buster was sitting by himself at the back of the class. Amelia and Jens were in front of him. Buster could see Jens's red pencils lying side by side in the three compartments of his pencil case (the case was a present from Jens's grandfather, who worked in a steam laundry in the Philippines). He could also see under Jens's desk, into the small, shallow drawer where Jens had fixed a yellow piece of paper with long lines of numbers on it.

Mr. Martinsen cleared his throat. He had the pile of exercise booklets in one hand.

"School exercise booklets," he announced, "all ought to look the same. They should have the owner's name and class written on them and nothing else. In capital letters." He put the exercise booklets down on the desk again. "I am glad to say most of you realize that. However, there are some among you who believe the covers of exercise booklets ought to resemble works of art. What, may I ask, do you think your booklet looks like when you've painted little figures on the back cover, Benny Lukas Johansen? As for Buster—Buster's exercise booklet is no longer gray. I might almost say it's all colors of the rainbow. Is it really necessary for your teacher to see the sun, moon, and stars every time he corrects your math problems, Buster Mortensen? In the future, exercise booklets will be gray—plain gray. Benny and Buster will make sure theirs look like all the others."

"Just like those milk cartons," remarked Buster to himself.

"What did you say, Buster?"

Mr. Martinsen was standing on tiptoe. That was a bad sign. It meant he was about to get worked up. Benny said it proved Mr. Martinsen had been a ballet dancer before he became a math teacher. Benny was probably right. At any rate, Mr. Martinsen could stand on tiptoe for a remarkably long time. Maybe he had once danced on stage in a tutu, with flowers in his hair.

"Something seems to be amusing you, Buster," said the math teacher.

"No, no," Buster hastened to assure him, "it was just because—well, milk cartons are all supposed to look the same, or no, not quite the same, or you couldn't tell the difference."

Mr. Martinsen stared at him.

"I mean, it's not right for the buttermilk to stick its tongue out," Buster hesitantly explained.

By now the whole class was staring at him. Mr. Martinsen came slowly up to his desk.

"What is that you're holding?" he asked with irritation.

Buster, who had never owned a pencil case in his life, was holding a ballpoint pen.

"Mr. Martinsen said we mustn't write in ballpoint, right?" said Jens, looking from Buster to Mr. Martinsen.

"And what way is that to hold a pen?" asked Mr. Martinsen.

Buster looked at the ballpoint pen. Its tip pointed upward. One half of the ballpoint pen was a small transparent plastic tube with a lady on it. She was standing in front of some green palm trees and wearing a red bathing suit.

"He probably hasn't got anything else to write with," said Amelia.

Buster looked at her and thought of her clever sister who knew the seventeen times table.

"Is that so, Buster Mortensen?" asked Mr. Martinsen.

Buster nodded.

Mr. Martinsen gave him his exercise booklet. "Write your name on the black line—in capital letters!"

Buster looked at the booklet, but he did not hold the ballpoint pen in the correct position for writing.

"Come on, what are you waiting for?" asked Mr. Martinsen. "Write your name!"

"In capital letters!" added Jens.

"Asta in the Brønshøj bar gave me the ballpoint pen," muttered Buster under his breath. "That's why."

"That's why what?"

Buster hunched his shoulders. "If I turn it the other way up something will happen."

This was too much for Mr. Martinsen. He

snatched the ballpoint pen from Buster's hand and wrote BUSTER in large, clear capital letters on the black line. Then he looked in some alarm at the ballpoint pen. The lady's bathing suit had quietly disappeared.

Buster tightened his lips and swept a bread crumb off the edge of the desk.

Mr. Martinsen put the ballpoint pen down and went back to his desk.

"Now then, move the desks so that you're sitting well apart. This is a test, and if I catch anyone helping somebody else, you will both get a zero to take home. Understand?"

Most of the children nodded. Buster smiled and said, "It's always nice to have a change."

Mr. Martinsen stared at him.

"A change, Buster Mortensen?"

"Yes," said Buster. "With Rosa we learn about Vikings, and we're supposed to help each other, or Rosa gets cross. But with you it's the other way around."

With three long strides Mr. Martinsen was right beside Buster. A little muscle had begun to twitch under each of his eyes, and he was giving a tremendous performance of his tiptoe trick.

"Now let me tell you something, Buster O. Mortensen. This is not play school, this is a foretaste of the realities of life. Once you're grown-up and you have to leave school and look after yourselves there will be no one to help you with anything. It's every man for himself then."

"Just like the Vikings," agreed Benny Lukas Johansen.

"Hold your tongue, Benny!" shouted Mr. Martinsen, bending over so that his back was hunched. He looked very peculiar hunching his back and standing on tiptoe at the same time.

"Out there," said Mr. Martinsen, pointing to the window, "out there you'll have no doting mothers to help you, understand? Out there you'll need to be strong, and if you want to be strong you'll have to know the things you were taught in school. In the old days, long, long ago, brute force was enough. But we don't need that kind of strength now; we need brains these days."

"My dad is a construction worker," said Benny.

Mr. Martinsen looked at him.

"He's ever so strong," explained Benny.

"Yes, but we don't need that kind of strength anymore, get it, fathead?" said Sarah, making a face.

"Stop that," said Mr. Martinsen. "Be quiet. That's not the point at all. What I'm telling you is, you've got to learn what you're taught in school if you want to make something of yourselves."

"Like Amelia's big sister," said Buster.

Amelia nodded smugly and cast her eyes downward. Mr. Martinsen asked what on earth Amelia's big sister had to do with anything.

"She knows her seventeen times table," Buster told him.

The other children looked at Amelia, much impressed. Sarah asked Amelia to walk home with her. Mr. Martinsen went to the sink in the corner of the room and took a long drink of water.

Then he said, "Put the desks back."

The children looked at each other, bewildered, and put the desks back.

"Now, you can take out your math books and go on where we left off."

At that moment there was a knock on the door. It was Kurt's father. He nodded to Mr. Martinsen and took a small box out of his pocket. "Sorry," he said. "Kurt forgot his retainer. Maybe I can help him fit it on his teeth."

Mr. Martinsen dropped onto his chair and looked at his watch. It was nine-thirty. A boy asked if he could eat the omelet he'd brought for recess right now, please, because otherwise it was going to get runny in his pocket, and a girl complained that Eric had taken her green fruit drops and fed them to the custodian's dog, and now the custodian's dog had a green tongue.

Meanwhile Jens folded up his list of numbers and asked Amelia if she wanted to come and listen to records after school, but Amelia said he was only saying that because of her big sister who knew her seventeen times table.

In the middle of all this, Buster went up to Mr. Martinsen and leaned confidentially over the desk.

"Do look out of the window, Mr. Martinsen," he said in a friendly tone. "The sun's stuck itself on the church flagpole, see? It looks like a red candy apple."

The math teacher sighed and looked out of the window. "Yes," he said, wearily. "Yes, you may be right."

Buster smiled, and all of a sudden Mr. Martinsen smiled too, and the next moment the lady who came to paint the children's teeth with fluoride walked through the door. Mr. Martinsen just sat there smiling while the children rinsed and gargled. Buster saw no good reason to go back to his desk. He stood there and rinsed his teeth, still smiling at the math teacher.

Then the bell rang. The children streamed out, and Mr. Martinsen collected the math books.

"I have a rehearsal this afternoon," said Buster, who had stayed behind.

"Yes?" sighed the math teacher.

"A rehearsal of the play about Sheikh Suleiman," Buster explained.

Mr. Martinsen went to the door, nodding at Buster.

"I have to move all the scenery," said Buster proudly.

"It's recess now," murmured Mr. Martinsen, making for the teachers' room.

Buster nodded and waved good-bye.

Outside, the sun had moved on, away from the flagpole.

CHAPTER SIX

A Dress Rehearsal

This was the first time the children had seen the stage in its full glory, with lights and curtains and scenery and all. They greatly admired the big backdrops and flats the custodian, cursing and swearing, had lugged into the gym. The performance was in another two weeks, so most of the actors were already very excited. The custodian, on the other hand, was firmly convinced that the school should not to be wasting time and money on such garbage. It ought to be teaching children something practical.

It would never have occurred to him to go to the theater himself. Night after night he sat and stared at the TV screen, which he switched on at seven-thirty sharp. "Kids these days have it too easy," he said whenever he passed a classroom where children were laughing or singing. And now he leaned against the wall and stared crossly at the twenty-five children who had come for the first dress rehearsal. After a bit, their hopping and dancing around was too much for him. In five furious strides he was next to Eric, whose face and chest were painted brown and whose hair was hidden by a white turban.

"What's all this supposed to be?" the custodian snarled.

Eric hitched up his baggy pants. "I'm one of Sheikh Suleiman's faithful henchmen," he answered proudly.

"Huh!" grunted the custodian, scratching his nose. "You kids got nothing better to do with your time than chase around with shoe polish all over your faces? Talk about mollycoddling you!"

Eric said it hadn't been easy for him to find time to be in the play, because he had a job stuffing ads through doors three times a week, and when he stayed with his dad in town on Fridays he had to help in his dad's shop.

The custodian scowled at Eric, then took his carton of sixty-watt bulbs to his room and listened to the news on the radio.

Meanwhile the music teacher, Willy Valdi, had told the music group to play something called an overture, which was the music that began the performance. Ingeborg had been practicing the difficult notes all week, and now she was so nervous her hands were sweaty. But maybe the others felt the same. There were several recorders, large and small, guitars and bongo drums, and Volmar's electric harmonica, supposedly invented by Volmar's father.

The electric harmonica had made Volmar quite famous when his picture appeared in the local paper. There was also a photograph of Bishop's Hill Cemetery, where Volmar's grandfather was buried. Actually, it was Volmar's grandfather who had invented the electronic harmonica, but when he switched on the current in the garage for the first time and put the instrument to his lips, there was some kind of short circuit. Volmar's grandmother didn't find his grandfather until late that evening when she went out to the garage to bring him a bowl of pea soup, and there lay Volmar's grandfather with the harmonica still in his mouth.

Volmar said that for some reason or other all his grandfather's hair had been standing on end. Luckily his father knew more about electricity, so now it was almost completely safe to play the electric harmonica.

The actors, who had rehearsed the play with the music teacher several times over the last few days, came on stage. Mr. Valdi showed them where and how to move.

"Everything you do has to be exaggerated," he said. "So even if you feel shy about it, you must act dramatically. Move your mouths a lot and open your eyes wide."

Everyone nodded.

When the curtains opened, the ladies of the harem—Anna, Amelia, and Sophie—were to enter from the right, dancing to the music of drums and recorders. Benny Lukas Johansen, back early from the silver anniversary in Åbenrå, was immediately given the job of pulling the curtains. He was to open them very slowly at a sign from the music teacher. At the same time, Bloodhound (whose real name was Knud) was to switch the lights off in the gym. Benny also had the job of throwing some sand onto the stage from a shoe box, to make the desert scene more realistic. He had brought the sand himself.

Everyone was in position when Buster, who had not yet found out what his job as a stagehand entailed, went up to the music teacher. "If there's nothing else for me to do in the first act I don't mind blowing into the microphone to make it sound like a sandstorm," he suggested to Mr. Valdi.

"We don't need any sandstorms, Buster," answered the music teacher. "If you just wait behind the big flat and make sure it's moved away before act two, that will be fine.''

The music teacher waved him away.

Then the curtains were opened for the first rehearsal in costume. Anna, Amelia, and Sophie danced in from the right. Buster saw Benny throw a handful of sand on the stage, at which point there was a great uproar. Anna cried and stamped her foot because she got sand in her eyes. Amelia said Benny should never have been asked to bring in the sand because he'd just emptied out his bird cage, and now bird droppings and feathers were all over everything.

"Yes, and I could easily get asthma from the birdseed," said Sophie. "This is the end, Benny!" So it was decided to forget about the desert sand. They hurried on to the second act. This was Buster's moment to push the heavy flat painted with desert scenery aside and drag in the next one, so that everything would be in place when the curtain went up on act 2.

Jens, playing Sheikh Suleiman, was standing behind Buster, straightening his moustache. Buster thought the moustache looked wonderfully dashing.

"It looks just like a real moustache, Jens," he said.

"Yes, but hurry up and get that scenery moved," replied Jens, smiling at Rosie. In a few minutes Rosie was due to be kidnapped by a boy from seventh grade called Oyvind. Then Jens was to rush in and fight furiously with Oyvind, and finally Rosie (playing Princess Goldilocks) was to escape with the sheikh, who would be badly wounded in one elbow. Together they would sing a song in a shady oasis.

"Everyone ready for the second act!" shouted the music teacher.

The drums rolled menacingly and the curtains opened as Buster clung to the flat showing a nighttime scene with two palm trees. All in all, it weighed sixty kilos. There were wooden supports at the side, but if someone didn't hold on to it the whole time, it wobbled. If even one actor leaned against a palm tree, the whole contraption might collapse.

Rosie glided in carrying a jug of water and sang:

>With a pitcher in my hand
>lonesome, all alone,
>I walk through the desert sand
>all, all alone.
>Oh, I love Sheikh Suleiman
>Suleiman
>Suleiman,

I bring him water in this can,
water sweet to drink.

When she sang *Suleiman* for the third time, Oyvind entered from the left holding a sharp knife. "Ha, ha, ha!" he laughed. "A beauteous maiden for the robber Cadabra! Ha, ha, ha . . ." But here the music teacher shouted, "Stop, stop, stop!" and clambered up on stage, saying Oyvind couldn't possibly keep his glasses on; they didn't look right.

Oyvind said he couldn't see a thing without his glasses—he had inherited his poor eyesight from his mother, who also suffered from an underarm rash, though he had been spared the rash. The music teacher, however, was quite sure Oyvind could manage without his glasses. There was a long discussion. Meanwhile Jens asked Buster why on earth he had dressed up in a costume when all he had to do was stand and hold the scenery.

Buster was wearing Ingeborg's red carnival pants tied at the ankles. He had drawn a beard around his mouth with burned cork and wrapped a dish towel around his head. Still clinging to the nighttime scenery, he said it was in case anyone in the audience happened to see him.

"Yes, but they won't. You'll be *behind* that flat the whole time," Jens scoffed.

But Buster said people always went backstage, and it would look silly if he was standing there in a pair of brown pants and an ordinary white shirt. It would seem as if he didn't really belong in the production. Jens answered that stagehands ought to wear their ordinary clothes, and he was about to say a whole lot more when act 2 began again. Rosie, who had got some chewing gum in her hair during the lull, swayed across the stage.

Buster could see Oyvind standing in the wings, blinking nervously and stumbling around for the spot where he was supposed to enter.

"Follow your nose," Buster whispered.

Oyvind glared at him. "Shut your trap, Benny," he hissed.

Buster decided that Oyvind's eyesight must really be terrible.

Rosie had now finished her song. Oyvind rushed onstage again.

"*HaHA!*" he snarled, staring nearsightedly at a palm tree that he obviously mistook for Princess Goldilocks. "A beauteous robbery for the maiden Cadabra!"

"No, no, no!" wailed the music teacher, sending a boy called Philip out of the gym for stuffing a handkerchief down Sarah's recorder to make it squeak. "Oyvind, your line goes: 'Ha, ha, ha, a beauteous maiden for the *robber* Cadabra!' "

"Sorry," said Oyvind, plodding offstage again.

The music teacher sighed.

"Once again. Music. Curtains. Lights . . ."

The drummers began. The spotlights were directed on stage. Buster clung to the heavy flat. Jens ate a piece of the nougat his grandmother had given him when she stopped by to admire him in his desert costume.

Rosie sang her song for the third time, and Oyvind jumped out and recited his line perfectly. Then he produced a rope, tied up Benny Lukas Johansen, and kissed him on the forehead.

The music teacher stopped the music and went wearily over to Oyvind, who was stroking Benny's hair while Benny asked what in the world was going on.

Finally it was decided that Oyvind could wear a mask that would hide his glasses. Then they went on to the scene with Sheikh Suleiman.

"And move that flat, Buster," shouted the music teacher. Buster heaved and hauled and finally managed to get the nighttime flat off the stage. His back and arms hurt a lot as he dragged in the even heavier flat painted with a cave scene. There was a row of little yellow light bulbs fixed behind it. When switched on, they shone through little holes and looked like stars. The effect was very pretty.

Now Jens came onstage and started bossing Eric and Maurice, who were swaggering around being silly. Then he sat on a cushion and pretended to smoke a hookah, until suddenly he jumped up, cupped a hand to his ear, and cried, "Hark! Do I not hear screaming from afar? It sounds like Princess Goldilocks. Alas, alas—tell me, ye distant stars, how can I save her?"

Jens had been rehearsing with his mother over the weekend, and he knew his whole part by heart. He clapped a hand artistically to his brow and approached a yellow star. Behind the flat, Buster had switched the lights on. Jens groaned so pitifully he went quite red in the face. "Alas, what am I to do?"

"Wet your pants and let it dry," whispered Buster.

Eric and Maurice giggled, but Jens tore off his moustache and stamped on it, saying he wasn't going to be in this play anymore if that idiot Buster Mortensen was allowed to stand behind a star making fun of everything. The music teacher came up and dragged Buster out, and Benny had to hold the piece of scenery instead.

"Did you really say that about his pants and let it dry?" Willy Valdi asked through clenched teeth.

Buster nodded.

"And it's not right for him to be in a costume when he isn't really in the play!" Jens added.

But the music teacher announced he wanted no more trouble. Opening night was in two weeks and there was no time to waste.

Jens, Eric, and Maurice took their places. Buster switched the stars back on, and the play began again. At last things went smoothly. The actors knew their parts, and the music stopped only when the plug to Volmar's harmonica fell out.

However, Buster had something to think about. Rosie had said that if he wanted to walk in the park tomorrow afternoon he could call for her at her parents' shop on Frederikssund Road.

Buster had simply stared at her, nodding. Five minutes later the rehearsal was over. The actors changed and went home. Buster's gaze followed Rosie for a long time, and then he got Charlie Mane and led him slowly out of the gym.

"Here, Mortensen," said the music teacher. "Aren't you a stagehand?"

"Er, yes."

"Then it's your job to clean up. We can't have all this sand left lying around."

Buster turned Charlie back again. The door closed behind the music teacher.

It was perfectly quiet. Outside, darkness was falling. Buster propped Charlie against the piano.

Then he climbed onto the stage and began sweeping up the sand. He simply poured it into his pockets. When he was through, he switched on the two big spotlights and stood in the middle of the stage, legs wide apart.

"Ha, ha!" he shouted into the darkness. "Ha ha, Charlie, as if Suleiman couldn't see you, ha, ha! Well, let them play their music and bang their drums. I shall cut that tiny piece of nougat into so many pieces even Amelia's big sister couldn't count them, and then . . . aha, then, little Rosie with the chewing gum in your hair, then I'll . . . I'll . . ."

Buster found himself staring at the custodian, who had entered the gym quiet as a mouse.

The custodian shook his head. "This is what they spend our taxes on!" he said. "Snotty, spoiled kids painting their faces black instead of doing something sensible. You mark my words, we'll all pay for this!"

Buster nodded and thought of Rosie.

"This stupid little country of Denmark is really going down the drain, that's what. But I'm not interfering, I've got my own business to worry about. Let 'em throw their money out the window, that's what I say!"

Buster collected Charlie. "Just like my grandfather, the Great Oregon," he said.

The custodian looked at him crossly. "What?"

"His money disappeared too," explained Buster. "These are magic trousers I'm wearing. My grandfather got them from an African he met in Naestved, and at once all his money turned to sand!"

"You kids need a few licks of the strap, telling such shocking lies!" snapped the custodian. "Hoping to fool a grown man too!"

Buster went right up to him. "But it's true, I'm afraid," he said. "Every time Grandfather put a coin in his pocket it turned to sand, poor man. I wouldn't put as much as five ore in these trouser pockets myself."

The custodian straightened up.

"You come over here, boy. Let me tell you, you can't fool me! I'm canny, I am. Now, you put this five-ore piece in your pocket, and I'll teach you to try such tricks on me. Young rascals, the lot of you!"

Buster sighed mournfully and took the coin, dropping it into his pocket. He nodded sadly, brought out a handful of sand, and sprinkled it at the custodian's feet.

Then he told Charlie "Giddyap!" and Charlie immediately galloped out of the gym, leaving the custodian standing there with his carton full of light bulbs and a little heap of sand.

CHAPTER SEVEN

A Skyfaring Frigate

Ingeborg looked at Buster, who was flipping the switch of the water heater over and over again.

"It's no good," she said, resigned. "It won't work. We'll just have to wash the dishes in cold water."

"It's been in a bad mood for a whole week now," muttered Buster.

"Water heaters don't get moods, Buster," replied Ingeborg, picking up a dish towel. "They just break."

Buster unfolded another dish towel and held it out in front of him.

"Ladies and gentlemen, distinguished guests! You are now about to see, before your very eyes, the disappearing act of a perfectly normal Danish dishwashing operation! This amazing trick will be performed by none other than Miss Ingeborg

Mortensen, named after a five-legged anteater in Norway that could whistle the Norwegian national anthem while walking on the tips of its toes. Come closer, come closer, ladies and gentlemen. See the lovely Ingeborg do her amazing trick with plates, glasses, and pans. Watch her juggle the dishwashing sponge without any safety net. . . ."

"Okay, okay," said Ingeborg. "If your hands went as fast as your tongue we'd be through with this in ten minutes flat!"

Buster jumped on a chair, brandishing his dish towel and a glass.

"And here she goes! Watch carefully—now she's putting the glasses in water, one by one, watch her with that brush, see the dirt vanish, see her red fingers, see her yellow ears, see her black nose. . . . You know something, ladies and gentlemen? I once knew a man who swallowed a whole table and spat out the legs afterward—and boy, you should see what Ingeborg here can do; now it's the plates—but, but, but this man, you should just have seen him swallow tables, although of course they were dining tables, ladies and gentlemen. . . ."

Buster's mother poked her head around the door. "If you could just keep quiet a moment,

Buster, the rest of us might get a word in edgeways! Here you are, Charlie's survived his operation. That eye's sewn back in place."

Buster jumped down from the chair and wiped the table and the stove.

"You missed those gravy spots," said Ingeborg, taking the dishcloth from him.

"They're not really spots, just sort of freckles," he said. "You're getting to be a good housewife," he added.

Ingeborg stopped wiping the stove for a moment and looked sharply at him. "For your information, I am not going to be any kind of housewife."

"Well, that's better than being a bad one," said Buster. "Personally, I'm going to have five wives when I'm grown-up and old enough to marry."

"I thought you were going to marry Elvira from the supermarket," said Ingeborg, giggling.

Buster nodded. "Counting her, it'll be five," he agreed. "I believe in Allah, you see."

Ingeborg closed the kitchen window. "Allah? Who's he?"

"Some kind of smart aleck in Arabia," said Buster. "And out there in Arabia men can have as many wives as they like. Allah said so."

"The poor women!" said Ingeborg. "You mean they actually go along with that?"

Buster nodded. They went into the living room, where their mother was darning socks while their father mended the sail of the ship he and Buster had been building.

Buster explained that the Arabs all lie down on a carpet in the morning, look the same way, and pray to Allah. "With bare feet," he added.

"You don't really believe that, do you?" inquired Ingeborg, taking her recorder out of its case.

But Mom said Buster was partly right. Muslims turn their faces toward Mecca when they pray because it's their holy city.

"Exactly," said Buster. "They're all wild about this Allah person who was such a wise guy."

Mom bit a thread off. "Allah is the name the Arabs call God," she explained.

Ingeborg looked at Buster with a mocking smile. "Buster said he was a smart aleck."

Mom and Dad looked at Buster and smiled.

"Well, I ought to know, seeing as I'm a Muslim myself," said Buster. "And I read this big fat book saying Allah was a wise guy."

His mother asked him to fetch the book. It turned out to be a book of fairy tales he had borrowed from the library. One of the stories was about an Eastern merchant. The merchant didn't describe Allah as a wise guy, but he did say Allah was wise, which is not exactly the same thing, as Buster's mother gently explained.

Ingeborg looked the other way and suppressed a giggle, but their mother was looking at Buster as he stared at his book. She thought of the letter that had come from school. The teachers thought Buster would be better off in a different school with smaller classes. In what was called a special school. It was true that he was not very good at math and Danish. He had particular difficulties with arithmetic. A little while ago his mother had looked in his arithmetic exercise booklet to see how he was doing. She had found some thick red lines on page fifty-nine drawn in by Mr. Martinsen. The exercise went: "Bo, Søren, and Peter have been given 40 centimeters of licorice stick by Søren's mother. They want to divide it in such a way that each boy gets the same length of licorice stick. How much will each have? Write the result in your exercise booklet to three decimal points."

Buster, who really did try hard with his homework, had written, "I think they ought to give Søren's mother 10 centimeters for herself, because it was really nice of her to give them that licorice. Then Peter, Bo, and Søren would each get 10 centimeters."

Mr. Martinsen had written the correct result at the bottom of the page: 13.333 centimeters.

Right now, Buster and his father were assembling their frigate. They had been working on that ship for two months, and at last they had reached the point where they could hoist the sails.

"The ship sails at midnight, on course for the farthest stars," announced Buster, beaming.

"Now we only need to put the green eyes on the figurehead," said his father. "They're very important. Without those we'll run aground."

Buster nodded gravely, resting his arm in the glue. They searched high and low for one of the eyes, and of course finally found it sticking to his elbow.

Ingeborg was practicing her recorder for the play, and Mom was getting ready for bed. She had to be up early in the morning for her job cleaning offices.

As she lay her head on the pillow she heard Dad and Buster casting off from Brønshøj. They were sailing far, far away, because theirs was an unusual ship. It had become an unusual ship when they read the instructions and found out it mustn't be put in water.

"It's obviously a skyfaring frigate," Buster's father had said.

So now they could sit for hours on board their sailing ship, eyes closed, having strange and wonderful adventures.

"I see the first star ahead," said Dad. "Hold your course due south, Steersman."

"I'm at the wheel," called Buster from the bridge.

Dad shivered. "It's cold up here, and it echoes when you speak."

"That's because we're in deep space, Captain!" explained Buster.

"How much longer must we sail on in this cold, Steersman?" asked Dad, beating his arms to keep warm.

"We'll have to make do with the cold gusts of wind blowing off the moon until the water heater's fixed," answered Buster. "And it's quite a ways yet to the blue morning star where time stands still."

"Is that where dreams are born, Steersman?"

"Aye, aye, sir—and now I see the light of the blue morning star, we're steering straight for the mouth of it, and you'll have to close your eyes for a few minutes because it shines so bright, no human soul can bear the sight of it. Anyway, the secret of the morning star mustn't be told, and if you're curious you'll have to spend the rest of your life in the dark."

Ingeborg looked at the pair of them on the sofa and gathered her things together. "Good night, you two sillybillies," she said, kissing her father on the cheek.

"Did I hear a little angel over to starboard?" asked Buster.

"A kiss from the prettiest little cherub you ever saw, Buster," laughed Dad.

Ingeborg blew out a couple of the candles and emptied her mother's ashtray.

"Why no kiss for the steersman?" asked Buster, turning the wheel.

"Because the steersman hasn't had a bath for a week," said Ingeborg, going to the door that led to the attic room.

"Nearly there!" shouted Buster. "Close your eyes, cross your fingers, and count up to ten in Bantu. Thirty seconds more and we'll be in the land of the thousand suns where all the galaxies meet. . . . Kiss the stars, Captain, get out your harmonica, and then we'll sing the old dream song and set sail for Hope Street again."

Dad walked along the gleaming silver rail to his cabin, where he found his shiny harmonica and cleaned the spit and dirt out of it. "Are you there, Steersman? Now let's see if we can wake the old gods. They must be somewhere around here."

Then the captain began playing a tune, and the steersman sang so loud that his mother had to stuff cotton in her ears.

When the stars shine clear
shining down on Hope Street,
in the silence of
the night

When the racing clouds
pass across the sky
like a flock of birds
in flight

I can feel the wind
blow my hat away,
the wild wind blowing near
and far.

Then I take off too
in the summer night
and sail away to land upon
a star.

So blow, wind, blow,
as we sail fast and free,
yes, blow, wind, blow
across the dreamland sea.

I will build a ship
with a thousand sails
and on my ship I'll sail
away.

And I dream
that it sails
home to Hope Street,
and if you want to come
you may.

Dad looked at Buster sitting on the arm of the sofa.

"How many years have you known that song, Buster?"

"Two," said Buster. "You wrote it that time I went playing music in the streets with you and Mr. Larsen."

Buster's father stood up. "I didn't write it myself," he said. "Your grandmother wrote it."

Buster went over to Charlie Mane. "Is it true what Ingeborg says, about Grandma being a Gypsy?"

His father laughed and shook his head. "No, not exactly. But when she was a young woman she did travel with a group of Gypsies. They went a long way, all the way to Hungary, and that's where Grandma learned to read a crystal ball."

"Didn't she ever go to school?" asked Buster.

Dad put the ship away in the cupboard. "No, never," he said. "Or not in the kind of school you go to now, anyway. But she learned reading and writing and arithmetic and all sorts of other useful things. Ah," sighed Dad, "those were the days."

Buster nodded and took Charlie over to the door and upstairs to the attic, where Ingeborg was sitting up in bed reading with a flashlight. She did that almost every evening—she thought books were better when you read them that way.

Just now Ingeborg was reading a story about a poor little girl whose parents were divorced. The girl lived with her mother in a derelict building in the center of a city, and on page twenty-three her mother jumped out the window and was run over. On page twenty-four it said the mother had committed suicide because her son, the girl's brother, had become a drug addict because of all the environmental pollution in the city. Next day the girl's father came. He had been out of work

for ages and made a little money putting up posters that advocated revolution. Ingeborg had read
this book at least ten times and knew the story
by heart. The whole book was very sad, and
since Ingeborg had trouble falling asleep, this was
her favorite book: She only had to read a few
pages before she felt really tired.

Now she pulled the blankets up and caught
sight of Buster down on the floor with his bottom
stuck in the air. At first she thought he was looking for something on the carpet, but then she
heard a peculiar murmuring.

". . . And make Dr. Nielsen find out that Jens
has nits, so Nurse Heidi has to shave his head,
and his mother's head too—and . . . oh well, you
know the rest of it. Yours sincerely, Buster in
Denmark."

Buster rose to his feet.

"Your evening prayers to the wise guy, I suppose," giggled Ingeborg.

"There's nothing to laugh about," replied
Buster, getting into bed.

Ingeborg turned the flashlight off, and now the
only glow in the room was the blue radiance of
the streetlight outside.

"Ingeborg, do you believe in God?" asked
Buster, after a while.

"You know I do."

"And little baby cherubs too?"

"Not cherubs, angels."

"You believe they have wings on their backs and they can fly?"

Ingeborg turned over in bed so that they were nose to nose.

"Yes, I do," she said peaceably.

Buster's face assumed a cunning expression.

"Where do angels nest, then?"

"Nest?"

"Yes, nest. I mean, they're a kind of bird, so maybe they lay eggs too."

Ingeborg turned over again.

"You don't know a single thing about God and the angels, Buster," she said. "All you ever did with your Children's Illustrated Bible was press beer-bottle labels flat in it—you never read it. Nobody knows what God and the angels look like, because Jesus is the only person who's ever seen them."

Buster shook his head. "Adam and Eve saw them too. So did Benny's sister Gurli."

"Gurli says she's seen God?" Ingeborg sounded as if she didn't believe it.

"Yes, she has a photo of him," said Buster calmly. "She went to Rome, where the pope lives, and there was a man with crutches selling pictures of God."

Ingeborg turned over once again. Her cheeks were red now, and Buster thought it would be nice if one of his wives looked like her.

"You mustn't believe such things, Buster," she said. "No one can see God. He just exists, like the sun and the rain and the moon."

"Benny says God plays the organ in church every Sunday," Buster told her.

"Your friend Benny tells terrible lies."

Buster was silent for a while. Then he asked, "Can God hear what everyone's thinking?"

Ingeborg nodded. "Everyone in the whole world."

"Without electricity or a telephone line?"

"Yes."

"Can he hear what I'm saying now?"

Ingeborg nodded again.

"Then I suppose a person could pray to him too?"

"Yes, of course. Didn't you just pray to Allah, though?"

"Well, yes," said Buster. "I want him to do that stuff for me, about Jens and the nits, and if God lends a hand too I could be sure it would work even if Allah happens to slip up."

"You can only have one God," said Ingeborg. "And I guess God has better things to do than give Jens nits. Good night, Buster. Sleep tight."

Buster waited for a while, and then he patted Charlie's head and wrapped himself in the covers.

In that case it's a good thing I can fall back on Allah, he thought.

CHAPTER EIGHT

Oaths

Buster galloped down Frederikssund Road. He was in a big hurry and kept spurring Charlie on. After school his father had asked him to buy a bag of frozen peas from the corner shop, but for reasons of his own Buster had gone to the super-market, only to discover that Elvira was not sitting at checkout counter 16. Instead, her place was occupied by a lady with a face like a boiled potato.

Buster knew that the cashiers sometimes went out through a door, maybe to drink coffee, but he just could not imagine Elvira sitting with those other women in orange, utterly different from her, drinking coffee and eating sugar-topped cookies. He thought she must have become invisible already and descended into the Underground Land, where her ugly smock changed into a long white robe with gleaming silver lacing. Perhaps she was already clipping tickets in the underground Bella Cinema dressed like this.

As a result, he had to wait over a quarter of an hour to pay for his frozen peas, and of course it took an extra long time today because everyone was paying by check and some people couldn't find the silly little pictures of themselves the cashier had to see, and when they finally did find them, it took them half the year to write out the checks.

Buster had arranged to meet Ingeborg outside the supermarket. She had gone to the florist's while he bought the frozen peas.

"Did you get a nice bunch?" he asked breathlessly as he came hopping out mounted on Charlie Mane.

"Are you crazy?" said Ingeborg. "You don't get much for five kroner in a florist's. Two white carnations. And you owe me another three, because I had to get a bit of greenery to go with them."

Buster opened the thin waxed paper a crack. Those flowers are worth the money, he thought. Rosie's sure to like them.

"What sort of shop do her parents have?" asked Ingeborg.

Buster pinned the paper together again.

"No idea," he said. "Maybe they sell candy, though—imagine that!"

Ingeborg shrugged her shoulders and crossed the street. She was on her way to Scouts and was wearing her uniform.

Buster turned and raced across the marketplace. On the way he studied the note Rosie had given him in school. In beautiful script, she had written, "Rosie Gormsen, 194 Frederikssund Road, 2700 Brønshøj." Buster stuffed the paper into his breast pocket and rode past the place where there had once been a big pet shop that sold parrots, tortoises, and little red plastic divers blowing bubbles on the bottom of a huge aquarium. Last year he had often stood outside with Ingeborg watching the fish and the snails that moved so slowly you couldn't see it happen.

For a while Buster's dearest wish was to own an angelfish, but nothing came of it. By the time they actually could afford a little aquarium and a fish, the pet shop had closed. Two weeks later a lot of large machinery had come along, and in no time a yellow gas station was there instead.

Buster often wondered what had become of all those creatures and their cages and the man who sold them. But you never find out the answer to that sort of question.

He patted Charlie's head, and they rode past number 190. Looking in the glass of a display window, he straightened his cap and brushed the worst of the dirt off his jeans. Then he rode on to number 194 at a gentle trot.

There were boxes and shelves outside number 194, and customers were going in and out. The shop was called The Bouquet, and it was very large. Buster paused a moment, looking at Charlie and the bag of frozen peas. Then he went in.

It was amazing. There were flowers everywhere—large flowers and small flowers, flowers of every color. There were big bunches of the same kind of flower, and there were bouquets of mixed varieties. Other flowers stood under plastic domes and looked as if they must be the rarest of all.

Buster took a deep breath. The place smelled of foreign lands. Of mountains and fresh air, but also of cemeteries and hospitals.

"Can I help you?"

Buster turned and looked up at a tall, thin lady with a curiously triangular head. He looked down again to see if her feet were in water, but of course they weren't. The lady's hair was blue. Buster thought it must have been made of cotton.

He waved his bunch of flowers and the now

nearly defrosted peas. "I'm looking . . . er . . . for Rosie. I wanted to—"

"Roses, yes, how many would you like?"

"Um—I said Rosie, not roses."

The lady looked at him and smiled.

Her teeth are made of china, he thought; she could wash them along with the dishes in the evening.

"Ah, Rosie," said the lady, letting one eye rove around the shop. "She's out behind, making up bouquets with the other girls. Come along!"

The lady disappeared through a curtain made of lengths of bamboo, which sounded African as they knocked together. Buster took hold of Charlie, stuck his bunch of flowers under his arm, and followed her. The room behind the shop turned out to be three times as big as the shop itself, and Buster took a deep breath as he saw at least thirty girls his own age looking at him from a long table covered with flowers. They were all moving their hands very fast, and they all wore rubber aprons and head scarves. After a moment he realized that they were humming a tune. It went to the rhythm of their swift movements. He thought they looked very sad, as if they were tired of something.

The triangular lady put a hand on his shoulder. The hand smelled of stagnant water. Buster hastily stepped aside as a familiar voice said, "Hi, Buster!"

Rosie had stood up, her lap still full of carnations. Bright red long-stemmed carnations. It struck Buster now that she always did look a little sad.

They went into the shop, where Rosie put the carnations in a brass bucket. Buster handed her the bag of frozen peas. "For you," he said.

"Oh, thank you," she said. "I love peas."

Buster nodded and stuffed his little bunch of flowers into an empty vase.

The lady with the triangular face came out to them. "Well, are you off now, Rosie?" she asked, smiling.

"Yes, I'm just going to put the—er—peas away. . . . I won't be a moment, Buster."

Rosie took her apron off. The lady looked at Buster, who had stuck Charlie under his arm.

"I expect you're acting with Rosie in the school play," she said, smiling and nipping a faded petal off a rose.

Buster cleared his throat. "Yes, I'm playing a stagehand."

Finally Rosie came back. "That must be your horse," she said seriously.

"Yes, this is Charlie Mane."

"Can he carry us both?"

"You bet!" said Buster, laughing. "Jump on and you'll soon see!"

And off they rode. Down Frederikssund Road, along Marigold Road, and around the ancient Council Rock, where Rosie asked Buster to stop so she could get her breath back.

"It's my asthma," she explained when they had finally reached the park and found a green bench. It was covered with duck droppings. Buster gave Rosie the only spot that was remotely clean, and he sat at the other end, where the oldest dirt was. So they were sitting several meters apart. Rosie told Buster a little about her asthma, which meant she couldn't run fast for very long. If she did, she had difficulty breathing; it was very annoying.

Buster told her about a man he knew with only three fingers. The other six had been cut off by a machine in a safety-pin factory.

"What about the last one?" asked Rosie.

Buster looked at her blankly. "Er . . . well . . . About the last one, I think it was like this: The man was born with ten fingers, but, er . . . the tenth was right up on his elbow and it soon fell off."

"Fell off?"

"Yes. It fell off. It was found under a swing in his kindergarten."

"But didn't they sew it back on again?"

Buster shook his head sadly. "They tried, but he kept pulling out the thread, and finally they gave up."

Rosie slowly moved closer to Buster and put her hand on his arm.

"Look into my eyes," she said.

Buster looked deep into her eyes.

"Do you swear by all you hold sacred you're not lying?"

"Yes," said Buster. "If I must."

"Then say after me: If I tell a lie may my legs melt in the fires of hell, may an ox weighing a thousand kilos tear out my insides and trample on them, may my tongue be tied in seventeen granny knots so I can never speak again, and may I eat nothing but liver sausage for the rest of my life—if I tell a lie."

Buster looked at the swings and seesaws. "I don't think I can remember all that," he murmured.

Rosie put her arm round his shoulders. "Then say: If I tell a lie I'll kiss the first girl I see three times."

Buster bit his upper lip. "If that story about the finger was a lie, I'll kiss the first girl I see three times."

92

For a moment it was quiet in Utterslev Park.

"Look at me," said Rosie.

Buster looked up.

"Were you lying?"

"Yes. I was lying," whispered Buster.

"That whole story was a lie?"

Buster nodded.

"Then you must pay the forfeit twice," said Rosie softly.

"Really?"

Rosie nodded and offered him her cheek. Buster took a deep breath and kissed her five times on the cheek and once on the mouth. Rosie looked at him gravely. "Why did you kiss me on the mouth?" she asked.

Buster cleared his throat, and realized that his jeans were damp from the duck droppings.

"Well," he said, "maybe you don't know about Saint Goggelus from the holy land of Mocca, but he was a very famous bassoon. That means someone who doesn't even say 'Ow!' when you stick a pin in him. Anyway, shortly before his death he wrote a book about swearing oaths. I happened to read this book, and it said on page seven hundred sixty-five that oaths about kissing only count if you kiss on the mouth the last time."

Rosie took her bubble gum out of her mouth. "Can you swear that, Buster Mortensen?"

Buster nodded, and swore.

"That was a lie, right?" asked Rosie.

"From beginning to end," said Buster, laughing, and wiping his mouth on the inside of his jacket.

CHAPTER NINE

Jensen's Dairy and Some Green Moisturizer

Jens's mother looked from Jens to Buster.

"Why does he have to go with you?" she whispered to Jens, jerking her head toward Buster, who had sat down in an armchair.

"Because," said Jens, stamping his foot.

Buster settled himself in the comfortable armchair and let his gaze wander around the big beautiful room, where everything had its place and nothing was lying untidily about. Jens's mother vacuumed the carpet every day except Sunday, when she baked cookies. Twice a week she polished the dining table until you could see your face in it. There were little clear glass animals everywhere, and Buster knew Jens's mother cleaned them with pipe cleaners. Over the sofa, which had its cushions beaten three times a week and turned every two weeks so that they would wear evenly, hung a large painting of three ducks flying up from the reeds. It looked as if they wanted to fly away from that expensive sofa too.

Buster looked at Jens's mother, who was wearing a yellow apron. There were red slippers on her feet, and her legs were fat, much too fat for a woman of her age. Perhaps there's a little girl deep down inside her crying for help, thought Buster. Otherwise she suited this neat, tidy room very well. You could see that she belonged with the gleaming furniture and the little glass animals with their angular edges.

"Is your family very rich?" he asked Jens when they finally set off.

"Yes, we're tremendously rich," said Jens. "My dad earns all the money. He sells houses and apartments. It brings in a lot."

"Doesn't your mother earn anything?"

Jens stopped outside the barber's window, where there were pictures of a number of young men with the kind of haircut Jens wanted.

"My mom just stays at home and cleans and cooks," said Jens. "You don't make any money that way."

They went into the barber's. It smelled of perfume and hair spray. Two teenage punks were going out, looking aloof. They were white around the ears and had identical haircuts.

Buster had never been in a real barber's

before. His mother always cut his hair at home. He stared at the barber hurrying about, sweeping up hair with a little brush and then putting the hair in a box. In fact there were two barbers, both wearing fancy light brown smocks. Music came from somewhere, radio music of course, to make the customers feel happy and relaxed.

Buster thought that it was nice of Jens to let him come along, even though in return he had to give Jens a chance with the Arabian lamp. They had struck their bargain after Danish in school, when Jens had told Buster that he happened to speak fluent Arabic, and that was why he had been chosen to play the part of Sheikh Suleiman.

"My grandfather got the lamp the first time he went to Arabia," Buster had said. "It has to be pitch-dark, and then you put the lamp on a table and sit in front of it. You have to put a bit of moisturizer on first, of course, so your skin doesn't peel off later. After ten minutes you look like a real Arab."

Jens was immediately eager to try the lamp. There were only three days to go before the big night, and he wanted to have really dark skin and look like a genuine sheikh. So they had made a deal. If Jens could have a turn with the lamp, Buster could go to the barbershop with him.

Buster sighed and watched Jens being wrapped

in a large cloth. Then the barber stuffed cotton around his neck to keep hairs from falling down his back. It was very quiet as the barber combed Jens's hair. Jens told the barber he wanted to have a haircut like those in the photos in the window. The barber nodded and picked up his long scissors. Soon afterward Jens's hair was falling to the floor.

Buster shut his eyes and imagined he was the one having his hair cut by a real barber. Then he thought of his walk home from school yesterday, when he had passed the old dairy. It had been quite a while since he had been in that neighborhood, and he was surprised to see the door to the dairy standing wide open. Even more peculiar was the fact that there was nothing in the window. The glass was all dusty, and that wasn't like Mrs. Jensen, who always used to say a dusty window was a poor reflection on a shopkeeper.

Buster went in and saw that the shelves and refrigerator cases were empty too. Here and there electric cables stuck out, like intestines sticking out of a body. At first he thought a thief had been at work, but you don't often hear, "Hand over your butter, margarine, and yogurt or I shoot!" No, there must be some other reason.

Buster went into the back room. Everything was empty there too, except for a single milk crate with Mr. Jensen sitting on it. That was all there was—the crate and Mr. Jensen. Mr. Jensen was not wearing his white overalls either, but a pair of dark trousers and a gray knitted pullover. Buster put Charlie Mane down and stole closer.

When Mr. Jensen looked up and saw him, Buster took his knitted cap off. The two of them stared at each other for a long time, and Buster thought Mr. Jensen seemed to have changed somehow. He looked neither cross nor cunning. Once in the spring, Buster remembered, Mr. Jensen had grimaced in a way that could sort of be taken for a smile. That was when Buster had done a conjuring trick with toothpicks and a handkerchief. But he didn't look quite like that now, either. He looked as if someone had asked him a question he didn't understand.

Just like Buster had looked when Mr. Martinsen asked him what x was, when $3y$ was 9 and $2x$ was double the sum of the two smallest prime numbers between 20 and 46. Buster didn't know the answer, but the worst of it was that he didn't understand why Mr. Martinsen was asking him.

"Hi, Mr. Jensen," he murmured.

The dairyman nodded slowly.

Buster came a step nearer and looked into the empty room behind the shop. Mr. Jensen, on the other hand, stayed where he was and kept staring ahead of him.

Buster looked at him sideways. "Where's all the stock gone?" he asked.

Mr. Jensen didn't answer. Buster gazed out the back door, where the delivery bike stood leaning against the steps. The valve on the back tire must have been stolen, or else the tire had a hole.

Buster put his hand on Mr. Jensen's back. Mr. Jensen seemed to jump, but then he looked up at Buster and tried to assume his familiar old cross expression. It didn't work too well.

"Where's Mrs. Jensen?"

"At work."

Buster looked into the dairyman's eyes. "At work where?"

"In the dairy department of the supermarket," murmured Mr. Jensen. "Five hundred liters of milk every single day. Imagine that, Buster. Five hundred liters."

"But what about your dairy here?" asked Buster, spreading his arms out.

Mr. Jensen rose to his feet, sighing.

"What dairy? You're now standing in Brønshøj's new real-estate office. Jensen's Dairy closed three weeks ago." Mr. Jensen looked sadly at the walls, where the paint was all that was left of his dairy. "At least I'm rid of all the worry now. Old cartons, sour milk, sour customers. But how come they can sell five hundred liters of milk every day up at that place? There's a lot of milk drunk here in Brønshøj."

Buster looked with interest at Mr. Jensen, who had put his hands in his pockets. He had never seen those hands idle before. In the old days, when he, Buster, was still working at the dairy, Mr. Jensen's hands were always busy with something.

"Does Mrs. Jensen wear one of those orange smocks?" he asked.

Mr. Jensen turned and looked at him.

"How the hell do I know what the old girl wears up there?" he growled. "I don't care. She minds her business, I mind mine. That's how it is. Let folk do as they like so long as they leave me in peace."

Buster nodded. "Like the custodian," he said.

Mr. Jensen looked at him. Buster explained that the custodian always said the same thing.

"Ho, ho," said Mr. Jensen. "A school custodian, sitting on his bottom all day, what does he have to complain of? But it's the same everywhere, people are always grumbling, won't do anything themselves, and then they're surprised this stupid little country's going bankrupt. You work your fingers to the bone for twenty-five years, and what good does it do you?"

Mr. Jensen closed the back door and bolted it. "Ah well, I reckon I've just been stupid," he said gloomily.

Buster went into the room which had once been the front of the store. "I'm not too clever myself," he said, smiling and picking up Charlie.

Mr. Jensen looked at him in surprise. Buster explained that going to school wasn't always easy.

"Then why the devil are you laughing?" growled Mr. Jensen.

Buster pulled the knitted cap back on his head. "Because I can't help it," he said, laughing.

Mr. Jensen bent down, put a bucket on the counter, and said he had just been to his summer garden outside the city, painting the fence green.

"Can I have the bucket?" asked Buster.

"What for?"

"I collect buckets."

Mr. Jensen gave him the bucket. "But be careful. There's a little of the paint left in it."

Buster smiled and went on looking at the dairyman, who finally scratched the back of his neck and made a movement of his mouth which could definitely pass for a smile.

"Aw, go on now, boy," he said.

"See you," said Buster, and he rode home on Charlie's back.

Buster opened his eyes. There stood Jens in front of him, smelling fantastic. The barber swept and swept, and Jens counted out the exact change. He looked as if his ears had been moved.

Buster and Jens left the shop. "Remember what you promised," Jens reminded him.

Buster nodded and led Jens to Mr. Larsen's garage on Hope Street. It was full of rusty tools and cotton rags for cleaning.

"We won't be disturbed here," said Buster, placing a rickety chair in front of the workbench.

Then he hauled out a big box with a hole in the middle of it and put it in front of Jens, who had been unbuttoning his shirt.

"You must close your eyes," said Buster. "The light is very strong."

Jens closed his eyes.

"And you must rub your face with moisturizer first. We don't want your skin peeling off."

"Let's get it over with," said Jens. "My mom's got hot chocolate waiting at home."

Buster hurried to close the garage door. That made it pitch-dark. He reached for a large bucket standing behind Jens and dipped a white rag in it.

"The moisturizer might make your skin feel a little tight," he explained, "but that will pass."

Jens wrinkled his nose as Buster spread the stuff over his face. After a couple of minutes it covered Jens from the top of his head to the collar of his shirt.

"And now we'll switch the Arabian lamp on," announced Buster. "Ready, Jens? Watch out, here comes the sacred light!"

Inside the box, he switched on Ingeborg's flashlight.

"I don't notice anything special happening," muttered Jens, turning his face this way and that to make sure he got the light all over it.

"That's good," said Buster.

"Come to think of it, why don't you use the lamp yourself and get to be as brown as an Arab?" asked Jens.

Buster cleared his throat. "Well, for one thing, I'm not acting in the play, and for another, the lamp only works if a person knows Arabic, like you do, Jens."

"What's that supposed to mean? Isn't it the same whatever language you speak?"

"No, a real Arabian lamp can't be fooled," explained Buster. "If I were to use it I might end up green in the face."

Jens got up. "My skin feels tight," he said.

"Then the treatment's over." Buster opened the garage door. Ingeborg and Mr. Larsen were sitting outside, sharing the newspaper.

"Come on out, Jens," said Buster. "And you'd better hurry, or your chocolate will get cold!"

Jens stepped out into the sunlight, blinking his eyes and making faces because of his tight skin.

Ingeborg and Mr. Larsen stared at him. As he headed down the street, Mr. Larsen went over to Buster.

"Buster," he said, "is that kid green in the face or not?"

"Well, yes," murmured Buster. "I'm afraid he is."

"And how on earth did he get to look like that?"

"Well, it's a long and complicated story, Mr. Larsen," said Buster sadly, "but the point of it is that Jens doesn't know Arabic after all."

Mr. Larsen stared as Buster galloped out of the garage on Charlie Mane.

CHAPTER TEN

A Birthday Disaster

Doza Rosa was standing with her back to the blackboard, on which someone had written in yellow chalk "Eric and Sarah are in love."

The question was, who had written those six dreadful words? Sarah was sitting at the back of the class crying. She had almost completely soaked Anna's and Amelia's handkerchiefs. Eric had been sent out into the corridor because he kept saying he hated all girls, particularly Sarah, and Sarah replied that Eric was the lowest life-form in the whole world—and in any other world, for that matter—and she was going to pull all his hair out the first chance she got. So it was clear to everyone that the words on the blackboard were true.

Anyway, Rosa did not think they ought to spend the whole lesson over a silly thing like this, because today was the principal's sixtieth birthday, and in twenty minutes they and all the other classes were going to meet in the gym, where the teachers and children and two representatives of the cleaning staff would present Mr. Schlutter with a bunch of long-stemmed red roses and a large porcelain figurine of two polar bears biting each other's throats. The play ought really to have been performed also, but it wasn't ready yet, and so the song the music teacher had written for the occasion had to be sung especially well. All the boys and girls had rehearsed it until they knew it by heart. The song was called "The School of Life," and it was sung to the tune of "Nymphs and Shepherds Come Away."

Rosa smiled. "Well," she said, "let's hope Mr. Schlutter stays in his office while we go into the gym, or it won't be a surprise. We have to go now. Be sure to keep as quiet as mice."

The children left the classroom on tiptoe. Asbjørn had even taken off his rubber boots. They filed into the gym, which was full of children and decorated with flags and garlands in honor of the day.

"Stand in twos," called Rosa, counting them. Three children were missing.

"Where are Hans, Buster, and Benny Lukas Johansen?"

Jens, who had been away from school yesterday because of the green paint on his face, appointed himself class spokesperson and made his way forward. "Hans went home with a stomachache. Benny's down in the detention room. He has another two hours because he put sawdust on Hans's liver-sausage sandwich."

"What about Buster?"

"Buster's in the toilet," called Eric, from the back.

Rosa shifted impatiently from one foot to the other. It would be really annoying if Buster came wandering in right in the middle of the ceremony and then claimed it was her fault because she was his teacher. But at that very moment she caught sight of him. He was grinning like a Halloween jack-o'-lantern and waving cheerfully at her.

"It's all okay now," he whispered as he found his place.

Rosa told him to be quiet, because the assistant principal was heading up to the lectern.

The assistant principal asked them for silence. The plan was for the children to strike up their song just as the principal appeared in the doorway, whereupon the chairman of the school board would say a few words and hand him the fighting polar bears.

"Do all the classes know what they have to do?" asked the assistant principal.

"Yes," shouted the children.

"Excellent. It's now two minutes to twelve. We've asked Mr. Schlutter to come to the gym at twelve precisely—of course, he doesn't know why." The assistant principal stepped down from the lectern.

A curious quiet fell over the whole assembly. The teachers looked at their watches. It would soon be twelve. In fact, most of the watches said it was two minutes past twelve. The principal must surely be on his way, for he was known as a man who valued punctuality second only to Albanian pencil sharpeners.

The music teacher cracked his knuckles one by one as he sat at the piano. He adjusted the piano stool. People began whispering and comparing watches. Seconds passed, but nothing happened. At six minutes past twelve Walter, from class 9A, was sent out because he kept belching. Now the youngest children were getting restless. Someone began to cry and say he wanted his mommy, and meanwhile the hands on the watches slipped toward ten past twelve.

Then Walter opened the door, whereupon the music teacher played an opening chord and five hundred children began singing at the top of their voices. The teachers were unable to stop them until the middle of the second verse. Everyone stared at Walter, who blushed bright red.

"Um . . . er," he said three times, looking down the middle aisle at the assistant principal, who was back propping himself up on the lectern.

"Er," said Walter. "Somebody's knocking."

Walter was known for saying peculiar things. Once he said "conceivably" for a whole month. So the teachers looked at him and shook their heads. The children whispered. Walter repeated that there was someone knocking, and when he said it for the third time Buster tried to attract the attention of Rosa, who had her back turned and was talking to the custodian's helper.

"What's the boy saying?" asked the assistant principal.

"He says someone's knocking," said Mr. Frandsen, the art teacher.

"The noise seems to be coming from the offices upstairs," Walter continued.

"The noise is coming from the offices upstairs," Mr. Frandsen relayed.

The assistant principal paced up and down at the other end of the gym.

By now Buster had gotten Rosa's attention.

"What is it?" she snapped.

"I thought someone would be going to get him," said Buster.

"Get whom, Buster?"

"The principal! That's why I locked his door from the outside."

"Well, you'd better go back to your place and . . . What did you just say?"

The whole class looked at Buster, who simply waved his arms rather wildly.

"We didn't want him to come down too soon, did we?" muttered Buster.

The children looked at him, openmouthed, eyes wide. Rosa turned around three times and then collided with Mr. Martinsen, who asked what was wrong.

"Buster Mortensen has gone and wrecked the whole birthday celebration," said Sarah, mincing no words.

Rosa whispered something to the math teacher, who clapped his hand over his mouth in horror.

And now all hell broke loose. Rosa rushed up to the assistant principal, who was shaking Walter, and the next moment they all disappeared.

Meanwhile Mr. Martinsen grabbed Buster, who was pressed up against a wall at the back of the gym, keeping well out of the way.

Mr. Martinsen was white around the mouth,

and his back was hunched. "You know what you are, Buster?" he growled with grim rage. "You know what you are? Nothing, that's what you are. Nothing. Absolutely nothing. Just you wait, you zero, you nil, you . . . you nothing!"

At that moment the doors opened. The principal and the assistant principal came in. Both of them were rather red in the face, and it was a while before it occurred to the children that they ought to start singing.

Buster, however, was banished to the school yard, where the rain was pouring down.

"And you can just stay there," snapped Mr. Martinsen, slamming the door.

Buster looked up at the sky. It was gray and extremely wet. The sound of singing came from the gym.

"I'm not nothing," muttered Buster.

He went to a bench and sat down.

After about half an hour the others came out of the gym. Jens went straight to Buster, together with Sarah and Anna.

"You're nothing," they shouted. "Nothing, zero, nil, you're nothing. . . ."

Buster pretended not to have heard them and watched the drops of rain hopping up and down in the school yard.

112

You're nothing,
little nil, little zero, nothing,
little nil, little zero, nothing,
nothing.

It turned into a song. The rain joined in, and even after the bell rang and all the children went back to their classrooms the words echoed on in Buster's mind. His lower lip was trembling, and his fingers were blue with cold.

"I'm going to slip upstairs and get Charlie without telling anyone," he whispered to himself, "and then I'm going home. Because I'm not nothing."

He hurried across the school yard and snuck into his classroom. He always left Charlie where they hung their coats. He rummaged among the raincoats, but there was no sign of Charlie. Perhaps he had taken him into the art room. Buster ran to the other end of the building, but Charlie wasn't in the art room, either.

I just hope they haven't thrown him out into the rain, same as me, thought Buster. But maybe they have. Maybe he's lying in a puddle somewhere. It will be bad for his eyes. They'll rust.

Buster ran back to the school yard, where it was raining even harder now, if possible. He looked in the kindergarten playground and the soccer field. Finally he ran around calling Charlie's name, although he knew quite well that Charlie couldn't hear him.

He leaned against the flagpole and wrung his cap out. Then he thought of the custodian's lost and found room. Maybe Charlie had been turned in there. Maybe he was lying there now, among the sweaty socks and old soccer shoes. He ran across the school yard to the custodian's red house and knocked. It was a whole minute before the custodian's wife opened the door.

"What is it?"

"Could I take a look in the lost and found?" stammered Buster, shivering with cold.

"My husband's eating his lunch. Is it important?"

Buster nodded. Water fell from the peak of his cap.

The door closed. After a while it opened again. The custodian stood there in his undershirt and suspenders. Buster stuck his tongue out and caught a few raindrops.

"What's so important a man can't even eat in peace?"

"I want to look in the lost and found."

"What for?"

Buster wiped his nose and gazed up at the custodian. "Charlie Mane."

One side of the custodian's mouth opened. "What's this garbage you're saying?"

"Charlie is kind of a horse," explained Buster quietly, demonstrating the way he rode Charlie.

The expression on the custodian's face changed. "You mean a broomstick with a bit of horsehair mattress over one end?"

"Yes, that's Charlie."

The custodian leaned against the door frame. "You know what that thing was like?" he asked softly, slowly licking his lower lip.

Buster shook his head.

"Alive, it was."

"Alive?" Buster's jaw dropped.

"That's right, alive. Full of lice, the whole disgusting mattress crawling with them."

"Yes, but . . . where is he?" asked Buster warily.

"We burned that garbage right away—what did you imagine, for pity's sake?"

Buster stared at the man. A long moment went by. Then the custodian's features blurred as if the rain had wiped them out. The school yard rose, tipped sideways. The playing field began swaying. Soon afterward the shops on Frederikssund Road were rushing by like a long express train. Sky and ground kept changing places. . . . The gulls could be heard screaming somewhere nearby, and now the park came into view. The park, with its green hills, where you could see the rain rushing down as if the sky were an ocean that had opened.

Buster ran and ran. Up one hill, down another. And he shouted with all the power in his lungs. "I'm Buster," he shouted into the rain, "I'm Buster. . . . I'm not nothing. And I'm not crying either—it's only the rain. I'm . . . I'm . . ."

CHAPTER ELEVEN

Opening Night

Ingeborg was standing in front of the big mirror that hung on the inside of the wardrobe door. Her long, fair hair was freshly washed, and after ten minutes' work with the big brush it gleamed like pure Alaskan gold. She gathered it at her neck, holding her barrette between her teeth. The problem was how high up to make her ponytail. She had tried various positions and was not yet satisfied. But now she simply had to decide, because it was time to leave.

Buster was downstairs in the kitchen, drawing his black beard on with a burned cork. The Mortensen family had drunk red wine with their meatballs yesterday especially so Buster would have a cork.

Ingeborg had borrowed a little blush from her mother and was carefully dabbing it on her cheekbones. She stepped back a bit in order to see herself in the full-length mirror. Her dress was new. Well, not entirely new, since it was made of an old summer dress of her mother's. The material itself was fourteen years old and had something to do with her mother and father's first meeting.

All these years the dress had hung in a plastic bag in the wardrobe, until one fine day Ingeborg had found it and fallen in love with it. It had a royal blue background with little pink flowers casually scattered over it. The sleeves of the new dress were wide, almost puff sleeves, and were tied at Ingeborg's wrists. She had embroidered the same little pink flowers, which she thought might be lilies, on her white socks. It was almost too cold to go out with bare legs, but she thought socks would still be all right. It wasn't far to school.

Ingeborg looked at the time. Almost ten to seven. Mr. Valdi had said they were to be there at seven, half an hour before the audience would arrive. She gave herself a last look, then closed the wardrobe.

At that moment Buster came clattering up the stairs. He was wearing his Arab costume, and in honor of the occasion his little pointed beard had been made larger, so that it covered most of his face. No one would have recognized him. There was some burned cork on his eyebrows too.

He looked at Ingeborg with beaming eyes. "Wow. You look great!" he said.

Ingeborg picked up her recorder case, but as she was about to leave he gave her a big kiss.

"Ha, ha," he said. "That was terrific!"

She stared at him. Then she quietly opened the wardrobe door again and looked at herself in the mirror, sighing.

"Hey, Ingeborg!" said Buster. "We ought to get moving."

She turned toward him. Most of his beard was smeared around her mouth.

"Hey, Ingeborg, you forgot to shave!" he laughed.

Ingeborg couldn't help laughing too, although it wasn't really funny.

"Ladies and gentlemen, we are sorry to say that today's performance has to be canceled because of a nasty case of Andalusian mountain fever, but never fear, ladies and gentlemen, we have arranged for the best possible substitute. We present the Bearded Lady, Ingeborg Mortensen, from Brønshøj!"

"You're completely crazy," said Ingeborg, sitting down at the bureau and pulling out the top drawer.

"Run down to Mom and get me some soap," she sighed.

Buster hurtled downstairs, shouting for soap.

Ingeborg looked at the ceiling and counted to ten.

While the musicians rehearsed, Willy Valdi inspected his company of actors in their costumes. Two nervous mothers were helping with last-minute details. Buster gave Jens's mother a friendly smile, but when she simply bared her teeth and snarled at him, he thought it best to slip behind a piece of scenery.

"In a quarter of an hour," began the music teacher, "this hall will be full to overflowing, and we won't be able to stop and iron out problems anymore. Now, all of you do exactly what you did at the last dress rehearsal. Oyvind, don't forget the mask with your glasses. Benny, for God's sake, don't throw sand at the girls. Buster"—and here the music teacher took a deep breath— "Buster, do us all a great favor and don't say a word during the entire performance. Just make sure that the flats are shifted at the right time, and we'll be more than grateful."

"And he's not to appear onstage, even if he is in costume!" said Jens.

The music teacher nodded and continued. "Mrs. Møller, the coffee lady from the teacher's room, is down in that little box following every word of the play. If you happen to forget your lines, look at her and she'll whisper them to you."

"She's what they call a prompter," explained Jens.

"Yes, that's right, Jens," nodded Willy Valdi.

At that moment Edgar, who played the guitar in the orchestra, came up and announced that Volmar had forgotten his extension thingy, so they couldn't reach the outlet for his what's-it.

The music teacher looked at him with grim fury.

"Edgar, kindly express yourself in a way that we can understand."

Edgar scratched his head.

"Well, Volmar went and left his extension cord for the what's-its-name, I mean harmonium thingy, at home, and without electricity it sounds like an injured frog. So we urgently need an electrical thingy. Get it?"

The music teacher stared at him, and Jens's mother asked for a glass of water. Finally Edgar was sent to the custodian for an extension cord.

This did not suit the custodian, who wanted to go play bingo and had not expected to have to work overtime. But at last an extension cord was found. At that point the school's regular supply teacher opened the doors.

People streamed in: pupils, parents, grandparents, brothers and sisters, as well as two members of the cleaning staff and the chairman of the school board, who had his little black notebook with him, because he wanted to keep track of what the school's money was being spent on. Finally Mr. Schlutter, the principal, and his wife arrived. They were to sit in the front row, where little cushions from the art room had been placed on the bench. Right behind them sat Jens's mother and his grandparents, all with their cameras at the ready.

Behind the curtains the ladies of the harem, Anna, Amelia, and Sophie, were getting ready. Amelia and Anna were cross with Sophie because she had insisted on being the first to enter, so Amelia had pulled Sophie's hair and messed it up. If Benny Lukas Johansen hadn't intervened, the three little dears would never have made a proper entrance.

"You'll all get thumped if you don't behave," he threatened.

Otherwise, however, everything was as it

122

should be. The rest of the actors stood ready in their fine costumes behind the flat Buster was to hold in place for the next quarter of an hour.

Slowly the lights went out and the audience fell silent. The music began. It sounded wonderful. Volmar's electric harmonica was particularly effective. At a sign from the music teacher Benny pulled the cord, and the curtains slid quietly open. To the accompaniment of exciting drum rhythms, Sophie, Anna, and Amelia, in that order, danced on stage.

Pleasantly surprised, the audience applauded, and the girls' veil dance went just as planned. Then the music suddenly stopped. The ladies of the harem continued undulating, while to the sound of Ingeborg's solo recorder, Princess Goldilocks—alias Rosie—entered right. The audience went "Ooh!" and "Aaah!" because she really did look lovely. Next moment there was a loud *Blop!* Blue sparks appeared above the musicians. For a moment Rosie and the three dancers stood there at a loss. Then Willy Valdi interrupted the show to announce that he was afraid there would have to be a short intermission, and he signaled to Benny to close the curtains.

It turned out that a fuse had blown in Volmar's harmonica. Changing it took three or four hectic minutes.

Buster glanced at Jens, who had gold fringe sewn to his pant legs. Jens was getting ready to make a snide remark about Buster's Arabian lamp when the harmonica was fixed and the curtains were drawn back—just in time for everyone to see Amelia step on Sophie's toes, which was not part of the veil dance.

However, the end of the first scene was very effective: The girls brought out three baskets full of paper flowers and threw them among the spectators, who were, naturally, surprised and delighted. The effect was slightly spoiled by the fact that some of the flowers were stuck into lumps of modeling clay, and they were rather hard if they happened to hit you on the head. Mrs. Schlutter changed places with a teacher in the second row after being struck on the forehead. By then, however, it was time for act 2.

The curtains slid aside just as Buster managed to push the heavy nighttime flat into place. Oyvind was getting ready in the wings. He was so nervous that he had trouble keeping both the mask and his glasses on his nose.

The drums started and Rosie glided on once more, singing her romantic song about the jug of water. As planned, the robber Cadabra, otherwise known as Oyvind, entered from the right as Rosie was in the middle of the third verse. Unfortunately, as he made his entrance he lost his mask and glasses and panicked, running in place for several seconds and peering nearsightedly at Mrs. Møller, who was anxiously flipping through the script.

"Ha ha," she whispered. "Ha, ha . . ."

"Er, ha, ha . . . A beauteous maiden for the robber Cadabra, ha, ha . . . er . . . ha, ha, ha!"

Rosie began whimpering in a very convincing way.

"Weeping won't help you, little desert oasis, my beautiful date palm, my intoxicating fig flower."

Oyvind drew his scimitar, which gleamed menacingly in the light. The audience got gooseflesh, and Oyvind stamped energetically on the floor of the stage.

He was now supposed to say, "I will flee with you until the desert sand covers the bedouin oasis, O beautiful princess." But for some reason he had completely frozen—perhaps because Benny had found the mask and was trying to pass it to him unobtrusively from the wings.

"Psst," whispered Benny. "Your glasses, Oyvind."

"Er . . . um . . ." stammered Oyvind, hopping sideways as the heat overcame him, "you intoxicating fig flower. . . ."

Meanwhile Mrs. Møller was whispering herself hoarse down in her box. "I will flee with you . . . Oyvind! . . . until the desert sand covers the bedouin oasis. . . ."

The music teacher chewed his knuckles and signaled to the drummers to play loudly. He tried to wave Benny off the stage.

Finally Oyvind got hold of Rosie and spoke clearly. "I will cover you with desert sand until it flees from the oasis, you lovely date. . . . er . . ."

A murmur ran through the rows of seats. Mrs. Møller pulled at her hair, and the music teacher raced up and started urging Oyvind off. All this time the school board chairman kept writing in his little black book.

"Curtains, curtains," the music teacher hissed at Benny. Oyvind, who was still on stage, started shouting "Curtains! Curtains!" too as he groped around for Rosie.

Finally Benny got the message and pulled the curtains so that Willy Valdi could go onstage and sort things out. Unfortunately, Oyvind chose this moment to utterly lose his sense of direction and wander out through the curtains, over the edge of the stage, and into the auditorium, where he staggered blindly around among the amused spectators.

After ten minutes it was possible to carry on

with the show, and it is fair to say that everyone breathed a sigh of relief as Sheikh Suleiman, otherwise known as Jens, entered with Maurice and Eric. All of them knew their parts perfectly, and it hardly mattered that the flash of Jens's mother's camera kept going off at the front of the stage, so that Eric finally had to ask her to go back to her seat.

The scene between the three of them went according to plan, and immediately afterward there was a fifteen-minute intermission.

Behind the curtain, preparations were being made for the beautiful scene at the oasis, where Jens and Rosie were to admire the starry sky. Buster pushed the big flat into place and switched on the stars and the yellow moon. The curtains opened again.

The sheikh and the princess lay elegantly reclining on soft cushions. The sheikh was smoking his hookah, while the princess hid behind her veil.

Buster was standing right behind Jens, watching the stage through a star.

"By Allah, what a beautiful evening hour!" said Jens. "But do not all the stars pale before the lovely face of Princess Goldilocks? Let me unveil that face, O beautiful Princess!"

"Eek!" said Rosie, hastily moving away from

the sheikh. "How do you know it would not be a mirage, a trick of the light and the air?"

Jens put his head back, laughed, and saw Buster's round head behind the third star on the left. Buster smiled at him, but Jens just stared furiously at the star and drew his scimitar.

"A mirage, did you say, O lovely one?" he snarled, pushing the sword backward through the star with Buster's head behind it. "No, no, you date palm of virtue, you lovely fig flower, you . . ."

Jens's scimitar went through the hole cut for the star, and Buster had to duck quickly to avoid being hit. Unfortunately, Jens's arm followed his sword through the hole, and it stuck there.

Onstage Rosie was saying her lines. Behind the flat, Buster was trying to twist Jens's arm free. Jens screamed in such a heartrending way that the audience spontaneously applauded his convincing performance.

"Oh, Princess Goldilocks . . . how I long . . . Aaaargh! . . . My heart will break in two. . . ."

Buster twisted the arm farther round, but it was obviously too much for Jens. In midsentence he screamed like a stuck pig, carrying on as if the end of the world had come. Benny drew the curtains without even being told to.

128

Next moment the music teacher was onstage, making straight for Jens and his arm.

"It's Buster's fault," hissed Jens. "He wrecks everything, that's what he does, he just wrecks everything."

They pulled and pushed at the arm, from in front, from behind, and from both sides. But it was as stuck as ever. Benny suggested chopping it off with the scimitar, but Maurice said that would mess up the whole stage.

"We'll have to go on to another scene," said the music teacher finally. "Push this flat away and we'll go on to the last act, where the sheikh fights Cadabra and dies in the arms of his beloved."

"What about my arm?" cried Jens.

Willy Valdi gave him a brief glance. "I know—we'll turn the flat here around and put a palm tree in front to hide your arm. That should solve the problem. You can hold the flat steady, Jens, and Buster will play Sheikh Suleiman in the last act."

There was deathly silence for a moment, and then Jens let out such a screech that out in the audience his mother gasped for air. Jens could not collapse entirely, however, because his arm was stuck in the star. Not only was he relegated to propping up the scenery in his new gold-embroidered costume, while his mother and grandparents sat in the second row with sixty color exposures still in their cameras, but Buster Oregon Mortensen was to play Sheikh Suleiman in the last act . . . with Rosie. It was just too much!

"I shall tear my costume!" wailed Jens, trying to stamp on Buster's toes. But just then Eric and Benny turned the flat, and Jens had to turn too if his arm was not to be wrenched again. Meanwhile someone wheeled on a palm tree to hide the arm.

Buster went over to Rosie. "Remember Saint Goggelus?" he whispered.

Rosie nodded, looking a little sad, as usual.

Finally the curtains parted again. The audience bravely applauded. The music struck up. Oyvind (wearing his mask and glasses this time) rushed in with his scimitar raised.

"Where's that vile sheikh? Now let him taste Cadabra's thirsty sword!"

Buster entered from the left, with the homemade scimitar that had once been a parsley chopper.

No one had stopped to considered whether he knew Jens's part—certainly not Buster, who couldn't care less what the text of the play actually said.

130

"Oho, so there you are, you slimy desert rat, you crumbling cookie, you cheap walk-on part!" shouted Buster dramatically, jumping up and down three times.

Oyvind stared speechlessly from Buster to the music teacher, who collapsed onto his piano stool.

"Come here, and let Mecca's sun not go down before one of us lies dead in the desert sand," muttered Oyvind.

"Aha!" cried Buster. "So he's playing dumb, as if Sheikh Suleiman didn't know how to fence, as if sword-fighting was difficult. Come here, you lousy lamp polisher, and prepare to meet your doom! My grandfather had a camel that got thumped on the hump every day, but you should just have seen the tent doors whipping in the wind in our camp, and true as my name is Suleiman, Allah is a real wise man, the wisest ever seen in Brønshøj, and let me tell you, I've often chopped the likes of you into little bits and sold them as licorice in a deserted dairy. . . . So just come here, my fine friend!"

Down in the prompter's box, Mrs. Møller went on grimly whispering, because at this point the sheikh was supposed to fall down and lie dying until Princess Goldilocks came to bid him farewell. Unfortunately, Oyvind was so carried away by Buster's shouting and yelling that he entirely forgot to stab him, and when Buster raced around the stage inventing more speeches, Mrs. Møller had to leave her box and remind Oyvind of his murderous duty.

"What, by Zeus?" cried Buster, removing the palm that concealed Jens's arm. "Another mirage—another trick of the light and air! Away with it, I say!" And he hit Jens on the fingers and would have done yet more damage to his poor hand, except Oyvind finally lunged at Buster, whispering, "Fall down and die, you bonehead!"

"Aaaargh!" wailed Buster, instantly falling to his knees. "I'm hit right in the middle of the synagogue under my ribs. Call my beloved, I'm seeing visions already, visions of arms hanging from twinkling stars, of five hundred liters of skim milk, ah, you evil robber, bring me my beloved, one last kiss before I see Mrs. Møller's cup of coffee for the last time, oooh, oooh, and three times oooh!"

Rosie sprang in from the wings. "Sheikh of all sheikhs," she wept, "I will die by your side! Let us go to the prophet together, far, far away, far, far away. . . ."

It was all extremely beautiful, and when the

lights were slowly dimmed and a lone flute played, the applause broke loose. The actors had to take their bows again and again, and Buster and Rosie each got a bouquet of carnations from the principal's wife. Buster remembered to put a flower in Jens's hand, so that at least he could have some share in the applause.

It was late as Ingeborg and Buster walked home down the dark neighborhood streets. Ingeborg went ahead, playing her recorder. Buster lagged behind, because he had to keep reenacting that last scene over and over, ending up dead on the sidewalk.

There was nothing but a pale moon in the black night sky, but stars shone in Buster's eyes as he followed Ingeborg into their building.

From the moon he looked small, very small, almost as small as the moon seems to be when you gaze up at it from Hope Street in the land of Denmark.

CHAPTER TWELVE

The Return
of Buster's Pointed Hat

Perhaps it was because it was Sunday—but in any event, the last remains of summer blazed up, inflaming the golden autumn season so that the leaves curled and dried, and people swarmed out into the sun to say a proper good-bye to it.

There were flags flying in the gardens, looking gay against the rather pale blue sky.

Mr. Larsen stood in front of the building on Hope Street. His hands were dug deep into his pockets and he was looking thoughtfully at the sky. Buster was with him, wearing his pointed conjuror's hat in honor of the fine weather. Besides, his knitted cap was in the wash.

"Well, there goes the last of summer on its tired old legs, Buster," sighed Mr. Larsen. "Winter's just around the corner. You notice these things when you get to be my age."

Buster looked at the ancient linden tree. "See that, Mr. Larsen?" he asked. "There's only one leaf left on the tree."

Mr. Larsen snorted and spat out something black. "Wait, Buster, the leaf will be gone tomorrow. We can expect only cold winds from now on, son. Well, I was on my way to see the wife." Mr. Larsen looked at Buster. "You don't want to come with me, I suppose?"

Buster nodded and pushed his hand into Mr. Larsen's rough but warm one.

Ten minutes later they were standing by Mrs. Larsen's grave in the cemetery.

As usual, Mr. Larsen had his little rake with him, and he didn't say much.

Buster watched two sparrows drinking from a dish of water and didn't notice Mr. Larsen looking sideways at him, smiling slightly. "You're very quiet today, Buster," he said. "That's not like you."

Buster just shrugged his shoulders.

Mr. Larsen nodded. "Come along, let's go," he said, "or we'll just be standing here till we're tired of standing."

But Buster held his hand firmly. "I know how you feel," he said.

"You do?"

Buster nodded, gravely. "I've lost someone I loved too."

Mr. Larsen bent down and looked at him.

"They burned Charlie Mane," Buster told him. "Because he was crawling with lice."

Mr. Larsen cleared his throat and put an arm around Buster's shoulders. Slowly, the two of them left the cemetery and walked to the marketplace, where Mr. Larsen stopped outside the door of the bar. He looked at Buster and smiled. Buster looked into space.

"Mr. Larsen, do you know the fairy Elvira?" he asked.

"The fairy Elvira?"

"Yes," said Buster. "Sometimes she sits in the supermarket, but mostly she collects movie tickets in the Underground Land."

Mr. Larsen looked at him. "Tell me about her," he said, taking Buster's hand again and walking past the bar. "And then we'll go home and see if that last leaf is still on the tree."

They crossed Frederikssund Road. Mr. Larsen listened, and Buster explained, but he had to hold on to his pointed hat the whole time.

To keep the cold wind from blowing it away.